Oh! Olivia

A Calico Cat Mystery

Book One

Parker Campbell glanced at her feline sidekick as she drove the familiar stretch of highway toward her childhood home. She shook her head in wonderment. *How can Olivia be comfortable in that crazy twisted position? And how can she sleep with my music blaring?* Parker chuckled and said to the cat, "Is that why you have your paw over your ear, Olivia? Is my music too loud?" She turned down the radio. "Yeah, it's even getting to me. Besides, we'll be on Gramma's street in a few minutes. Don't want to scare her neighbors or wake up anyone from their afternoon nap."

Olivia rolled over onto her stomach and blinked her gold-green eyes. "Yes, we're almost there, aren't we?" Parker said, running her hand over the calico's silky fur. "You always know." She grinned when Olivia sat up in her car seat and peered out through the windows. "Don't get too excited, sweet girl; Gramma's probably still at work. I'm pretty sure we'll have the house to ourselves for an hour or so." She yawned. "Maybe I can get a nap before things become crazy around there." She nodded. "That's right, *crazy*. Your Uncle Wade will be there, and maybe your Grandpa and Gail. Who knows what neighbors might drop by with desserts? Gramma's neighbors are always bringing her sweet things, especially this time of year. I'm glad I don't live closer; it's hard enough maintaining my waistline, if you'd call it that." She glanced down at herself and sighed. "Yeah, I need to put myself on a stricter and healthier diet."

Parker thought back to their recent stay in Northern California with the Ivey family and let out a deep sigh. "Especially if I want a figure like Savannah's." She muttered, "Like that will ever happen. She's tall and svelte. I'm, well, not as tall and not as svelte. It is what it is, Olivia. Remember that."

When Olivia struggled to break loose from her restraint Parker soothed, "Just settle down, little girl. I'll unfasten your seat belt in a minute. See, we're almost there. Olivia," she scolded, "stop biting your seat belt. Just relax, will you? What are you so excited about, anyway? Do you need to use the litter box?" She frowned. "Oh, I'm sorry. We haven't stopped for a potty break, have we? Well, here we are—home for Christmas." She pulled into the driveway of her mother's modest Malibu home, turned off the engine, and unfastened the cat's

Oh! Olivia

A Calico Cat Mystery

Patricia Fry

Oh! Olivia

A Calico Cat Mystery
by Patricia Fry

copyright © 2021 Patricia Fry

ISBN 978-1-7369430-0-7

Cover Art: Bernadette E. Kazmarski

Cover layout: Dennis Mullican
Page layout: Dennis Mullican

Printed in U.S.A. by: KDP

restraint. She snapped the leash to Olivia's harness and stepped out of the car. "Come on, Livvie," she said, expecting the cat to follow.

Instead, Olivia climbed out of her car seat, sat down on the driver's seat, and sniffed the air that wafted into the car.

Parker chuckled. "Do you smell the ocean, girl? Yeah, it's not too far away. Maybe we'll walk down to the beach while we're here. You can ride in your backpack. You like your backpack if there's a reward at the end of the ride, right? Like a frolic on the beach." More impatiently, she said, "Well, come on. Do you want to go potty or not?"

Olivia remained seated, her ears rotating inquisitively.

"What?" Parker cranked. "Do you want to be carried? Is that it?" She reached for the calico and received a soft paw-slap. "Now, what's that about?" she huffed. "You don't slap Mommy."

Just then she heard another voice. "I'll bet she does whatever she darn well pleases."

Parker looked up and greeted one of her mother's closest neighbors. "Donny, hello."

He tried to see through the windows of Parker's Jeep SUV. "I assume that's the gorgeous redhead you're talking to—the cute cat that Alejandro fell in love with last summer."

Parker thought for a moment. "Oh, yes, your Maine coon cat." She laughed. "I'd forgotten about their summer romance." Olivia emitted a series of high-pitched mews, and Parker said, "Yeah, you two were quite enthralled with each other, weren't you?'

"Speak of the devil," Donny said, motioning toward his fluffy tabby cat. "Here he is, eager to reunite with his girlfriend." He followed Alejandro around to the other side of the car and watched as the cat pushed past Parker and attempted to greet her feline passenger. When Olivia hissed, Donny quickly picked up Alejandro, saying, "Oh, buddy, I think you're coming on a little strong there. The pretty girl probably needs time to freshen up after her trip."

Parker laughed and ruffled the fur around Olivia's neck. "So true. I'll give her time to get settled, then maybe you can bring Alejandro over to the deck out back for a visit." She glanced toward Donny's house. "Love your Christmas decorations, but then, you always do it up big for holidays. I'll bet Cecilia's day-care kids love it."

Donny nodded and frowned. "Actually…"

"Is something wrong?" Parker asked.

"I hope not, but…" Donny started. He glanced behind him. "Here come the police now. I'd better go talk to them."

"Is Cecilia okay?" Parker asked, concerned.

He took a deep breath. "Yeah, she's just a little frazzled. One of the kids is missing. I'm sure he's just hiding someplace in the house. He does that sometimes, but she's pretty worried because we can't find him anywhere. He hasn't jumped out to surprise us like he usually does. I thought we knew all of his hiding places."

"Oh no. How long has he been missing?" Parker asked.

"Maybe fifteen minutes. Like I said, he does this, but today…" Donny moved closer and lowered his voice. "Cecilia was kind of worried about him before this happened. She even called me at the office to ask if I thought he might have been drugged or something. I handed my last two patients over to my associate so I could come home and take a look at him, but by the time I arrived he was already missing." When Donny saw two officers get out of the squad car, he said, "Hey, gotta go. I'm sure we'll see you later."

"Let me know if there's anything I can do," she called. She thought, *I should have offered to take Olivia over there. He probably doesn't know about her unique ability to find missing persons.* She looked at the calico, who now had her paws on the dashboard and was sniffing the crystal that hung from the rearview mirror. *She does have that unique ability, but only when it suits her. I sure don't want to promise something that we can't deliver, or that might delay the search. I'll check with Cecilia in a bit to see if they need help.* She stared after Donny, then urged Olivia to jump down out of the car, saying, "Well, I guess you don't need to go potty. Let's get you inside, then I'll bring in the rest of our stuff." She glanced toward the neighbor's house again, picked up her purse, tote bag, and the cup of coffee she'd been nursing, and closed the car door. "No!" she called when the cat pulled against the leash. "Olivia, you made me spill my coffee. Darn it." She placed the dripping cup on the hood of her car and struggled to get a better grip on the leash, but it was too late. The cat was off and running. "Olivia!" she shouted, almost certain she would be ignored.

Just then she heard someone call out, "Did you find him?"

Parker glanced around and saw a pair of eyes peering at her from over the fence next door. "Did I find him?" she repeated, puzzled.

"I thought I heard you call his name," the man said. He stood up on something so he could see into her mother's yard. That's when Parker saw the uniform.

"You're a policeman," she observed. "You're looking for the missing child. No, I haven't seen him." She clumsily dropped her tote bag onto the ground next to her car, slung her purse across her shoulders, and explained, "I was calling my cat. She just got away from me."

"I thought you called Oliver's name," the officer explained.

"No, Olivia," Parker said. "The boy's name is Oliver?"

He nodded, then looked around Parker's mother's yard before saying, "Well, thank you. Let us know if you see the child, will you?"

"Sure will," she agreed.

He started to step down, then asked, "If we run out of options over here we may want to…"

"You think he might have wandered over here?" Parker asked. "Sure. Feel free to look around if you want." She took a few steps along the path toward her mother's backyard. "I'd better go see where my cat went." She looked up just in time to see the leash disappear over the gate. "Darn it," she complained, jogging to the gate and opening it. "Olivia!" she called, glancing around the yard. Again, she realized how fruitless it was to call her, and again, the leash revealed Olivia's whereabouts. "Oh great," she complained. "Yeah, go under the house and get filthy, Olivia. That's what we need. Mom isn't crazy about all the fur you shed on her furniture as it is." She approached the crawl space under the house. "And you're going to cause me to get all dirty too, aren't you?" When she saw the crawl hole grate lying aside she grinned. "Well, not this time, you little stinker." She fitted the grate over the crawl space, made sure it was secure, then stood up and brushed the dirt off her pants legs. Feeling a tad smug for having won a battle with her devious diva cat, she said, "You just stay there for now. I'll deal with you after I've unloaded our stuff. You're no help, anyway," she muttered, walking back to her car.

Parker had closed the gate behind her when she heard someone say, "Talking to yourself again?"

She smiled brightly. "Wade!" she called, running to hug him. "You're early. I didn't think you'd pull in until sometime tonight." She looked around. "How'd you get here? Where's your truck?"

"I took it to my favorite mechanic to get an oil change and a couple of other things done. I've been here all day waiting for you. Where've you been?"

"Dillydallying, mostly," Parker said. "If I'd known…" she started. She tilted her head. "You've been here all day?"

"Well, maybe for an hour," he said, grinning. "Or twenty minutes." He glanced down at her feet and into the car. "Where's Patches?"

"Her name's not Patches," she asserted. "It's Olivia." She grimaced. "Although there are times when that ragamuffin name fits her." She added, "I read once that it's a good idea to name a child or a pet something you envision them becoming—I wanted Olivia to be more aristocratic—you know, refined and sophisticated." She wrinkled her nose. "Patches is a commonplace name. It's what you'd *expect* someone to name a calico cat or a pinto pony

8

or maybe an Australian shepherd. It's cute, but mundane and predictable."

He picked up her bag. "Are you saying I'm mundane and predictable?"

"Anything but," she said, grinning mischievously. "However, your name choices…"

"Where is she?" he asked again. "You didn't sell her, did you? Or did you forget to put her in the car?"

She gasped in jest. "Oh no. I forgot Olivia!"

"Really?" he asked, aghast.

"No, silly." She opened the back of her car and motioned toward a litter box and a shopping bag of litter and canned cat food. "Want to carry that in for me? Give me the tote, and I'll grab my overnight bag."

He looked into the cargo space at a large suitcase, a duffle bag, and a garment bag. "How long are you planning to stay here?"

"Huh? Oh," she said, "just a couple of days, then I'm off on an assignment." She waved a hand dismissively. "I'll tell you about it later."

"So where is she?" Wade asked again, placing the shopping bag into the litter tray and lifting it out of the car.

"She got away from me," Parker explained. More smugly, she said, "I closed her under the house."

"Then who's that?" he asked, walking out from behind the car.

"Olivia!" Parker exclaimed, dropping the overnight bag and grabbing the cat's leash. "How did you…? You little Houdini."

"I thought you said you closed her under the house," Wade needled.

"I did," she insisted. More uncertain now, she said, "At least I blocked one exit. There may be others that I don't know about." Holding tightly to the leash, Parker awkwardly reached for her overnight bag.

"I'll get it," Wade said, rearranging the load he carried and picking it up. He grinned down at the cat. "Looks like you have your hands full there with that aristocratic cat of yours."

Parker smirked playfully at him, then looked down at Olivia. "Let's go get you settled, you naughty girl."

"Yeah, that's Patches," Wade confirmed.

"That was a more Patches-like behavior for sure," Parker agreed. She chuckled. "I guess we could make Patches her middle name."

"She has a first and last name?" Wade teased. "What's her last name?"

"Campbell, of course," she said.

He grinned. "Why does she need a last name? Does she have a passport?" He followed Parker and Olivia through the front door of their mother's house, saying, "I never understood why you took our stepfather's name when you already had a perfectly good last name. Were you mad at Dad or something? You know, I think that hurt his feelings."

Parker turned to face him. "I don't think so. He said he was okay with it." More energetically she said, "In fact, he agreed with me that Parker Campbell was a stronger name than Parker Colton." She tilted her head. "Now, Wade Colton, that works. But I had…"

"I know," Wade said, "aspirations. You wanted to see your name in lights and on billboards."

"No, I did not," she countered, "just as a byline in magazines and maybe on book covers."

He grinned at her, then asked, "Where do you want the princess's toilet?"

Parker gazed around the large living room, which was decorated in a crazy mix of traditional beach décor and French provincial pieces that had been in the family forever. "Fresh fruit," she said, dropping her things and gravitating toward the kitchen. She ran her hand over the large dining room table before plucking an apple from a basket. "Mom always has a bowl of fresh fruit. To this day, I'm a fruitaholic."

"I found something better than that," Wade said. He pointed. "Those coconut cookies one of her neighbors makes and chocolate brownies."

"Yum," she said, rubbing the apple against her jacket sleeve. She took a bite, danced into the spacious kitchen, and spun around. "I love coming home, don't you?"

Wade balanced the litter tray on the back of a sofa. "Yeah, but remember this wasn't my home growing up, just like Dad's and Gail's place wasn't your home."

She faced him. "I felt at home there when I visited."

"Yeah, that's just it, you were a visitor, just like I was a visitor here after the divorce, when I moved with Dad into his quarters at the thoroughbred ranch."

She stared at him for a moment, then walked back into the living room. "Well, we're both visitors here now." She asked, "Which room did you take?"

"The one I always take—the red-and-blue room with the dartboard." He asked, "Will you be staying in your princess room upstairs?"

"I guess," she said. "Yeah, let's unload this stuff up there. Come on, I want to see if I still have that wide ocean view."

"There's an ocean view from the deck," Wade reminded her.

"Still?" She looked out through the glass patio doors. "Yeah, just a sliver."

"Why would you think the view would disappear?" he asked, following her up the stairs.

"Because of trees growing bigger and people adding on to their homes and obstructing the view," she explained. She walked into her childhood room, placed her things on the bed, and opened the drapes. "Yes!" she exclaimed. "It's even clear enough today that you can see it. If it's foggy, forget it. You'd never know you lived in a beach community, except for the sand you sweep up every day." She frowned. "I hated sweeping up sand all the time."

"Maybe it's angel dust," Wade said. When Parker looked confused, he chuckled. "You're just looking at it all wrong. Consider it angel dust and it becomes something magical instead of a nuisance."

She shook her head. "Leave it to you to make lemonade."

"Speaking of lemonade," he said, turning to leave the room, "want something to drink?" He stopped abruptly. "Oops, I almost collided with your cat. Hey, aren't you going to take off her leash?"

"Yeah, you can take it off her. Hey, I'd better fill her litter box and unpack a few things." She asked, "So what do we have to drink?" When Olivia strutted toward her, Parker picked her up and snuggled with her. "I was enjoying a cup of coffee, but Olivia made me spill it." She ran her hand over the cat's fur. "Or was that Patches?"

Wade chuckled, then recited, "We have coffee, tea, beer, some sort of lemon drink, red wine…"

"What are you having?" she asked.
"A beer."

"Sounds good," Parker said. "We'll be down in a minute. Want to sit out on the deck and soak up the last of the sunshine?"

Wade nodded and walked out of the room.

"What took you so long?" he asked when Parker joined him in the kitchen with Olivia, who was still wearing her harness. "Did you iron all your clothes and hang them up, take a shower, do your hair, groom the cat?"

"I wasn't gone that long. Anyway, I wanted to set up Olivia's comfort station."

Wade guffawed. "Comfort station? What is she, a baby? Isn't that what they call those diaper-changing tables in public restrooms, comfort stations?"

"Yeah, well, her litter box, water bowl, kibbles…"

"All in the same area?" Wade asked, surprised.

"No," she assured him. "Her toilet is in the bathroom. I'll feed her in the bedroom."

Wade nodded toward Olivia. "She wants to go out. It doesn't look like she wants to use her comfort station," he said, using finger quotes.

Parker put her hands on her hips. "Are you going to make fun of me these whole two days, because if you are…"

"No," he said, grinning, "just part of the time."

14

She shook her head and walked toward the patio door, then turned. "Well, two can play that game, you know."

He laughed eerily, saying, "Ohhh, I'm shaking in my boots."

She started to open the door, then walked away, saying, "I'd better get Olivia's leash." When she heard the door open behind her, she shouted, "Wait!" but she wasn't fast enough.

"What?" Wade asked, standing in the doorway.

"You just let my cat out, you knucklehead." She pushed past him. "Olivia! Olivia!" she called, trotting across the deck and down the steps after her. "Come on, sweet girl. Olivia!"

"What are you doing, Par-Par?" Wade asked, following her. "Do you really think she'll respond to that caterwauling?"

"Par-Par," someone repeated. "Do you know how long it's been since I've heard that?"

"Mom!" Wade said, jogging back up onto the deck. He wrapped his arms around her, and lifted her off the ground, then stepped back. "Just getting home from work? Hey, when are you going to retire and start having some fun, anyway? You know, you aren't getting any younger."

"Thanks for reminding me," Elaine Campbell huffed.

"Hi, Mom. Merry Christmas," Parker greeted, also hugging her. "You ought to own that

15

feed store by now. How long have you been there, anyway?"

"Going on twenty years," Elaine admitted. "I'm happy there, kids. It's an interesting job, I like the clientele and the aromas—you know, hay and grain, and I get to play with baby bunnies and ducks."

"Just as long as you're happy," Wade said. "'Cause the minute you're not, you need to quit. You don't have to work, you know. Greg left you a nice cushion to retire on."

"I know," Elaine said. "Retirement's for old people. It'll be a long time before I'll admit to being old." She looked at Wade. "Did Parker tell you I'm going to cut back to part-time?"

Parker grinned sheepishly. "Yeah, tell him why, Mom."

"So you'll have more time to play?" he asked.

"No. So she can work even more hours," Parker said.

"What's going on?" Wade asked, frowning.

When Elaine didn't speak right away, Parker announced, "She's now working two jobs."

"What?" Wade bellowed.

"It's not really work," Elaine said, "it'll be fun. It's something I've wanted to do for a long time."

"What, Mom?" he asked, suspiciously.

"I'll be working with a friend in her party-planning business. We'll do children's birthday parties, graduation parties, showers, *quinceaneras*, even office and company parties."

"I'm really happy for you, Mom," Parker said. "You've always had that knack for entertaining, and you do love a party."

Wade shook his head. "A real party-mama, huh?"

Eager to get the focus off herself, Elaine clapped her hands together, glanced around, and asked, "Okay, where's my grandcat?"

"Your what?" Wade questioned.

"Olivia." Elaine looked at Parker. "You brought her, didn't you?"

"Of course," Parker said, "but the stinker has gotten away from me twice already. I just saw her go under the house again. Those grate cover things were off. I put one back on, but then she discovered another opening over there." She strained to look at it, saying, "I'm watching for her to come out. Why were those covers off like that, Mom?"

"I don't know," Elaine said. "I had workmen here doing a few repairs last week. Maybe they went under there to check the pipes or something and forgot to put those back."

"I can do repairs for you, Mom," Wade said. "I told you to make a list of things you want done while I'm here. Why did you go and hire someone?"

"Because I want to spend quality time with you, not watch you work while you're here." Elaine walked with Parker to the crawl space opening and peered inside. "So that beautiful cat went in there with all the spiders and mouse droppings?"

Parker nodded. "If she doesn't come out in a few minutes, I'll see if I can lure her out." She grinned at Wade. "Or maybe I can bribe my brother to go in after her."

"You go get your own cat," Wade teased. "You're the tomboy in the family."

"Was," Parker insisted. "I *was* a tomboy."

Elaine leaned closer, and asked more quietly, "Does anyone know what's going on at Donny's and Cecilia's? I saw a police car out front."

Wade shook his head. "I didn't see anything."

"Yes," Parker said, wide-eyed, "they're looking for one of the day-care children. A little boy named Oliver. Are the police still there? Gads, he's been missing for a while now." She glanced at the neighboring house. "Maybe they found him, and they're interrogating him."

"Interrogating a child?" Elaine repeated.

"Well, calming him down or something. You know, talking to him," she explained.

When they heard someone else speak, they turned to see a policeman standing at the gate.

"Oh, hello," Elaine called. "I trust you've found the little boy."

18

"No, ma'am," he said. "I wonder if he could have opened the gates and wandered into your yard." He nodded slightly, and introduced himself. "Officer Spencer. Are you the homeowner?"

Elaine nodded. "I'm Elaine Campbell." She motioned to her left. "My son, Wade, and my daughter, Parker."

"So you didn't find him in the house?" Parker asked. She thought of something. "Hey, do they have a lazy Susan cabinet in the kitchen?"

"Ma'am?" the policeman responded.

"I've known of small children taking a ride on the spinning shelf, getting off in the back of it, and maybe falling asleep. Or he might have crawled in behind a deep drawer like those under a closet. Did you check the clothes dryer?"

"You must have kids," the policeman said, "adventurous kids."

"She *was* one," Elaine said under her breath.

Parker grinned at her mother, then explained, "No kids, but I have a curious and imaginative cat, and I'm an investigative reporter. I report on strange and difficult cases." She added, "Oh, and once we found a child hiding in the wheel well of an old boat trailer the neighbors had stored with a bunch of other junk on their property." She nodded toward the crawl space opening. "My cat actually found that little guy." Suddenly remembering, she said, "She also found a little girl in a filing cabinet." When the others waited to hear more, she explained, "Yeah, she climbed into one of those large filing cabinets and got closed inside."

The policeman stared at her for a few seconds, then asked, "Do you mind if we look around over here?"

Certainly not," Elaine said. "Please, help yourself."

He glanced across the yard, then walked closer to a large oak tree and peered up into it from different angles. He started to walk toward a small shed at the back of the property when he saw Parker on her hands and knees at the crawl space. He asked, "What are you doing there?"

She sighed deeply. "Still trying to get my hands on my wayward cat."

He watched her for a moment, then asked, "Mrs. Campbell, whose property is that on the other side of you? Is that your barn out there?"

Elaine shook her head. "We sold it to an out-of-town investor. So far, he just uses the barn for storage and pays someone to keep the weeds down."

"Do you happen to have a key to the place," he asked, "you know, in case of fire or something?"

Elaine nodded. "Yes, but I seriously doubt a small child could make his way onto that property. It's quite secure." When the officer continued gazing in that direction, she offered, "I'll be glad to open it up for you, though."

"Thanks," he said. "The mother's on her way here now. I want to talk to her, then we'll most likely expand our search to include the rest of your property."

The trio watched as the officer walked away. When Parker returned her attention to the crawl space, Wade offered, "Sis, let me get you a light."

"Thanks, Way-Way."

Elaine laughed and patted Wade on the back.

"What?" he asked.

"I just love having my Way-Way and Par-Par home, that's all." She added, "There's a flashlight on the kitchen counter near the coffee pot." She joined Parker at the crawl space again, saying, "I can't wait to get my hands on Miss Olivia. Olivia!" she called, "Gramma's here! Come see Gramma, baby girl."

"There she is," Parker said, using the flashlight Wade had handed her. Oh yes, this is a big help, it's dark under there. Olivia!" she called. "Please come out of there. I'm not in the mood to give you another bath."

"*Another* bath?" Wade questioned, chuckling.

"Yeah, on our way home from Hammond the other day, I stopped off to say hi to Aunt Sharlene and to let Olivia stretch her legs. Well, Aunt Sharlie wanted to take Olivia out to see all those cats she keeps in her outdoor run. She thought they might remember each other from the big family gathering she hosted last summer. So we walked out with her, and doggone if Olivia didn't find the only muddy spot on the entire property. I guess a hose was leaking or Aunt Sharlie was running the water for some reason, but before either of us knew what had happened, Olivia was a muddy mess. She actually might have been chasing a lizard. She seemed as surprised to find herself all muddy as we were. And she wasn't particularly happy with her bath that time. I think she still had her mind on that lizard, or she was embarrassed because all those other cats saw her little accident."

"Yup, Patches," Wade said.

"Patches?" Elaine repeated.

"He keeps disputing Olivia's name," Parker complained. "He thinks it should be Patches."

"Oh," Elaine looked under the house at Olivia again. "So, how are you going to get her out of there? Treats? Do you need treats? I think I still have those I bought for her last time you were here."

"Let me see where she is," Wade said, taking the flashlight from Parker. Before he could get in position to see Olivia, they heard wailing coming from Donny's and Cecilia's yard.

"My baby, my baby," a woman cried. "How long's he been gone? How could you let this happen? Did someone take him? Oh my God. Oh my God. Where's my baby?"

They could hear a man speaking quietly to the distraught woman, attempting to calm her, but she seemed inconsolable, demanding in a shrill voice, "Did you people do something to him to make him run away? He doesn't do that, you know, unless he's provoked. Wait!" she shouted. "He got mad at me once and he went into the garage and hid under the car. Boy, did he have hell to pay that time. He made me late for a luncheon. Did you check your garage? What about neighbors' garages?"

Wade winced at the woman's tone, then he got down on his stomach and focused intently into the light beam. After a few moments he said, "Par-Par, I think Olivia may be living up to her name at this very moment."

"What?" Parker asked. "Why? What's she doing?"

"Look," he said, making room for her.

"All I see," Parker said, disgustedly, "is my beautiful cat curled up with a pile of greasy rags, maybe, or someone's laundry." She asked, "Mom, are you missing any clothes? It looks like a packrat has carted off some of your things and made a nest under the house." She pulled back and shuddered. "Ewww. Wade, can you go in there and get Olivia? I don't want some animal biting her."

Wade grinned, then stood up and walked across the yard to the far fence.

"Wade," Parker called, "what are you doing? Are you going to make me go in after her? Please, Wade," she begged.

"It's okay," he said, motioning for his sister to calm down. He called over the fence, "Officer!" When Officer Spencer came closer, Wade said more quietly, "I think we've found the boy."

"My son?" the woman shrieked. "You have him over there? Why? Did you lure him with candy or something? Officer," she demanded, "arrest those people. They have my son."

"Ma'am," the officer said, "will you just please relax and stop jumping to conclusions?"

The second policeman walked around to the gate and let himself into Elaine's yard. He shook hands with Wade, saying, "Officer Baldwin."

"Wade Colton," he said. "The boy's under the house."

"So do you hear him crying under there?" the officer asked. "Is that how you found him?"

Wade kneeled at the crawl space, shined the light in, and said, "No. We haven't heard a peep. We were looking for my sister's cat. It appears that she's keeping the lad company," Wade said, "or it's the other way around."

"Well, I'll be," Officer Baldwin said, after scrutinizing the form lying next to the cat. He called out, "Spencer, bring the boy's mother over here, would you?"

"Where is he?" the woman demanded moments later, glancing around Elaine's yard. "My baby, where is he?" She scowled. "You know, he'd better be here, and he'd better have a good explanation for doing this to me. I had to take time off work. I have a dinner date tonight, and if I have to cancel because of that little jerk, well, I'll...I don't know what I'll do, but it won't be pretty."

Officer Spencer glanced at the others and shook his head disgustedly.

"Well, where is he?" the woman demanded.

"Over here," Officer Baldwin called. "Come down here next to me, and I'll shine the light in there for you."

"In the dirt?" she complained. "I told you I have a dinner date."

The officer looked pleadingly at Elaine, who said, "I'll get something for you to kneel on."

Once the woman was situated, the officer shined his light into the space and asked, "Do you see the cat? We presume that's your son with him. We can't see much except the clothing. Can you tell us if that's what he wore to day care today?"

The woman nodded. "I think so. Yeah, he has a shirt that color. What's wrong with him?" she asked, gasping. "Is he? He looks..." She looked again. "What's that cat doing? Why is Ollie under there with a cat? He'd better damn well not be scratching or biting my son." She looked at the others. "Whose cat is that? Is it a stray?" She peered under the house again. "He isn't moving. My son isn't moving. What has the cat done to him?" She looked back at the others again, "I heard that a cat can suck the breath right out of a child. Or did one of you harm him and hide him under there?" She continued ranting, "You know, I can smell a lawsuit coming. If that boy's dead, I'll have the lot of you arrested." She glanced around at the property. "And I'll sue you for every penny you've got."

Officer Baldwin shook his head, then called into the crawl space, "Oliver! Oliver, your mama's here. Time to wake up, Oliver."

"You're not going to get him awake that way," the woman said. "He sleeps a lot, and he sleeps soundly."

"That's what my wife says," Donny muttered, having wandered over from next door.

Officer Spencer looked at him. "Well, it seems abnormal for a three-year-old to sleep so much." He frowned, then said, "I'll get my overalls and go in under there." Minutes later, he located the opening nearest to the boy, scooted underneath the house, and crawled to where Olivia kept watch over the child. "Oliver," he said. He shook the child. "Oliver, wake up. Your mommy wants to see you."

The boy blinked and shook his head. "No," he said, rolling over toward Olivia. He put his arm around the cat, and pushed his face into her fur.

Officer Spencer petted Olivia. "Been taking care of the tyke, have you? Well, let's get both of

26

you out of here, shall we? Come on, cat," he called as he crawled on his elbows toward the opening with the boy resting in his arms. Olivia walked alongside the pair until she came up with a better idea. She climbed onto the officer's back and lay down. He chuckled. "Well, what's this, kitty-cat? Gonna ride out, are you? Don't want to get your feet dirty?"

As soon as the officer emerged with the child and his furry passenger, Parker scooped up Olivia and walked with her into the house. The woman screeched, "Ollie," and tried to pluck the boy from the officer's arms.

Officer Spencer turned away, saying, "I want to get a look at him." He called out, "Can someone bring me a blanket to lay him on?" Elaine ran into the house, returning with a quilt. The officer said, "Just lay it out there on the grass in the shade." He lowered the boy onto the quilt, saying, "I don't like the way he looks." He squinted up at the child's mother. "Has he been sick?"

The woman shook her head. "No. He just likes to sleep, is all. Let me take him home now and put him to bed." She glanced at her watch. "I still might be able to make my dinner date."

By then, Wade had secured all the crawl-space covers, and Parker had returned from the house with Olivia, her leash attached. When Parker lowered the cat to the deck, Olivia reached up with her paws against her leg. Parker kneeled and petted her, crooning, "What is it, sweetie?"

That's when Olivia rested one paw on Parker's thigh, swished her tail slowly from side to side, and quietly mewed.

"Show me, Olivia," Parker said, standing up. She followed the calico to where the boy lay, then watched as Olivia sniffed the child's head. She blurted, "I think he has a head injury."

Wade moved closer and whispered to his sister, "Yup, Olivia's with us today." He ruffled the fur on the cat's head. "Good job, girl."

"What?" the boy's mother shrieked.

"Look at that knot on his head," Parker said.

"A knot?" Officer Spencer asked.

"See where my cat's sniffing?" Parker said. "It looks like the boy banged his head on something."

The officer nodded. "Oh, I see that now. You have to look at it in a certain light."

"The cat told you that?" the toddler's mother questioned sarcastically. She moved closer. "I don't see anything. You people are crazy."

"I noticed that when he arrived this morning," Cecilia said, joining the others. "I actually mentioned it to his mother, didn't I, Arianna?"

"You did not," the woman declared. "He was perfectly fine when I dropped him off this morning. What did you people do to him?"

"Listen, lady," Officer Spencer said, "rather than stand there and argue, don't you think we'd better see if we can figure out what's wrong with your son?"

"He's fine," Arianna said, snatching him up and walking away with him.

Officer Baldwin stepped in front of her. "I'm afraid we'll have to insist that you wait with us for the paramedics."

"No," Arianna said, walking toward the gate. The officer blocked her exit, and she shouted, "Let me go. I…um…I have to pick up my daughter from school."

Officer Spencer looked at his watch. "This late in the day?"

"She had to stay over to…um…help the teacher with something. Listen, my son is fine. He just needs his rest. If you don't let me leave, I'll…"

"You'll what," Officer Baldwin asked, "call the police?" More seriously, he said, "I think you'd better wait here. Your son, ma'am, appears to be going in and out of consciousness. The paramedics are on the way."

"No!" she said, struggling to hold on to Oliver as Officer Baldwin eased him out of her arms. She protested as he carefully laid the child on the quilt and covered him up.

He calmly asked the woman, "Can you make arrangements for someone to pick up your other child? I think you should stay here with your son." When Arianna ignored him, he turned to Donny and Cecilia. "Do you know where her daughter goes to school?"

Cecilia shook her head, walked closer, and spoke more quietly. "As far as I know she doesn't have custody of her daughter. I used to take care of both children, but her daughter was put into a foster home." She leaned closer to the officer. "I'm awfully glad that you're getting involved. I think something's terribly wrong. I'd be happy to speak with the medical personnel about things I've noticed with Oliver most recently."

"Doesn't she take him to a doctor?" Elaine asked.

Cecilia shrugged. "Who knows? Every time that woman speaks, a different story comes out of her mouth." She motioned toward the gate. "The paramedics are here."

Officer Spencer greeted them and explained quietly, "The boy's been missing for thirty minutes or so. We just found him under the house with a cat, and he seems to be going in and out of consciousness." He nodded toward Olivia. "The cat pointed out what appears to be a contusion on his head. We agree it looks suspicious."

Wade stepped forward, "Yeah, it could be a head injury or maybe a growth or something affecting his brain."

"Are you a doctor?" the male paramedic asked.

30

Slightly embarrassed, Wade shook his head. He offered his hand. "No, I'm not. The name's Wade."

"Perry," the paramedic said, shaking Wade's hand. He nodded toward his partner. "That's Jennie." He asked, "Now, why do you say that?"

"It's just that I saw something like this once with a filly." When Perry appeared unconvinced, Wade said, "The thing is, my sister's cat..."

Jennie grinned. "The cat's a doctor?"

"No, but Olivia has been known to make some pretty mind-blowing diagnoses..." Wade started.

"The cat?" Perry exclaimed. He kneeled next to the child.

Jennie joined him and grinned. "Tell your cat thanks."

"She's my sister, Parker's cat," Wade said, shaking his head at the couple's somewhat condescending behavior.

"Wait," Perry said, more enthusiastically, "Parker Campbell? Are you talking about Parker Campbell's cat, Olivia?"

Wade nodded. "One and the same."

"Why didn't you say so, man?" Perry said. "Tell us more."

"Well, it's just that Olivia is rarely wrong and..."

"I know, I know," Perry said. He glanced around. "Say, is Parker Campbell here?"

Wade nodded.

"And Olivia?" he asked. "So Olivia made a diagnosis? Yeah, we'll definitely check for a head injury."

"Great," Wade said. "I only mention it because it's such a small contusion that I was afraid it might be overlooked, and since Olivia seemed…"

"Got it," Perry said.

Wade watched as Jennie examined the boy. When he saw Perry hanging back, he asked, "So how do you know my sister and her cat?"

He gazed at the boy and his partner, then said, "I don't have time to tell the whole story, but I happened to be at the scene of a car accident out on Pacific Coast Highway once, and a woman kept trying to tell us something about her grandfather, who was hurt. She spoke some foreign language that I didn't understand. No one around there knew what she was saying. Each time we'd prepare to lift the man into the ambulance, she'd start this gibberish. I'd already read some of Parker Campbell's articles, and I was a fan. So here she comes out of the crowd of bystanders with that cat—you know, Olivia. Ms. Campbell asked if she could let the cat maybe interpret for us. If it was anyone else, I would have had them hauled off to the loony farm, but it was Parker Campbell, so I said, 'Sure, give it a try.' Doggone if the cat didn't walk over to the guy, sit down and lay a paw on his right side. The distraught woman pointed and nodded. We checked the area and discovered that the man had a stimulator implant for pain, which was important for us to know about before subjecting him to some of the tests that would be in his future. Yeah, I'm a believer in the powers or instincts of that cat."

Chapter Two

"Is the princess all cleaned up?" Elaine asked when Parker walked into the living room a while later.

Olivia trotted along in front of her.

"You mean the queen?" Wade said. He tickled the fur around Olivia's neck. "Huh, Queenie?" He picked her up.

Parker warned, "She's still damp."

"Did you enjoy your bath?" he asked the cat.

"Always," Parker said, returning from the kitchen with a glass of water. "Well, almost always." She blew out a breath. "Whew, what a day. I don't know about you, Wade, but I come here to get away from the drama."

Elaine laughed. "Are you kidding? You bring it with you—both of you do. Every time you come here something oddball happens."

"Like what?" Wade challenged, watching Olivia step onto the coffee table and begin smoothing her fur with her tongue. He laughed. "That tail of hers—it's like it has a mind of its own."

Everyone watched as Olivia grabbed her fluffy tail and rather fiercely held it down while licking it.

Parker chuckled. "Yeah, it does aggravate her sometimes. You should see some of the battles she has with it." She looked at her mother. "You started to tell us about oddball happenings."

Elaine shifted in her chair and spoke to Wade. "Yes, like the time you brought a horse with you, and the neighbors called the cops because they couldn't sleep with that horse banging around in the trailer all night."

"He wasn't in the trailer all night," Wade said. "I pulled in around midnight, as I recall, and I delivered him to his new owner before daylight."

"Yes, but you still got a reprimand for disturbing the peace," Elaine said.

Parker laughed, then asked, "How long did you leave the poor horse in the trailer?"

"I took him out when I got here and walked him up and down the street a few times."

"And the sound of the shovel scooping up his leavings woke up neighbors on the next street over," Elaine complained. She looked at her daughter. "And you—remember the time you and Houston came with that litter of kittens you'd found at a rest stop on your way back from Oklahoma?"

Parker nodded. "Your neighbors loved them. We were able to place all four of them in good homes by the time we left."

"Really?" Wade asked.

Elaine leaned toward him. "Yes. Would you believe they enticed the neighborhood children with those kittens? How could the parents say no? One woman was actually mad at me until the family had spent a few weeks with the kitten." She chuckled. "She absolutely fell in love with that cat. I still see some of those cats around the neighborhood." She tilted her head. "Parker, how is Houston? Where is he this week?"

"Nevada," Parker said. "He was at my place for the last few days. We'll meet up in San Francisco in a couple of weeks and spend some time together before he heads back to Texas for a big rodeo there."

Elaine stared at her daughter for a moment. "When are you two going to get married and settle down like normal people?"

"They aren't normal people, Mom," Wade said.

Elaine shook her head. "None of you three are. Darn it, I want grandbabies!"

"Three?" Parker questioned.

"You, Houston, and Wade," Elaine clarified. "You're all unconventional."

Parker picked up Olivia and walked toward Elaine. "Mom," she said, mischievously, "you have a grandbaby. Here's your grandcat."

Elaine took the cat from her. "I do love Olivia. She's delightful, but I want human babies too, not just cats, goats, chickens, horses, and mules, for heaven's sake."

Parker and Wade laughed. He asked, "So, Sis, what will you be doing in Frisco? And I don't want the sordid details of your tryst with Houston."

"Tryst?" she repeated. "Where did that come from? Have you been reading the dictionary?"

He grinned impishly at her.

"For your information," Parker said, "Olivia and I have an interesting assignment in the city. And Mom, that's one reason why Houston and I haven't married yet. We will, but we both have things we want to accomplish first. I'm not finished making a difference in the world of crime fighting and the world of cats. There's a lot more work out there for Olivia and me to do in both areas. These are my passions. I can't imagine being bothered to take care of a home and a husband. Not yet. One day, but not yet." She added, "And Houston hasn't ridden his last bronc. Rodeo, as you know, is *his* passion."

"What's the interesting case in Frisco?" Wade asked.

"Cats galore, for one thing," Parker said. "I've been commissioned to do a piece on a group of ladies who care for perhaps the oldest cat colony in the area or the state, even. They're known as the Ladies of the Street Cats." She giggled. "When I told Savannah that, she thought I'd be interviewing prostitutes." She sat up straighter in her chair.

"Oh…oh, and Savannah took me to a cat ranch that is the absolute perfect model for cats like these. I may be able to share what I learned in Hammond with the women in San Francisco—you know, help them to create a safer environment for the feral cats in their colony."

"So no crime this time?" Wade asked. "Don't you usually write about criminal cases?"

Eyes wide, she said, "Oh yes—possibly. These cats seem to be dredging up things thought to belong to missing persons. So yes, there's every element that I love here—mystery, a possible crime, and cats. I'll have the opportunity to maybe teach and mentor these gals in creating a safer environment for the cats as well as help resolve a long-standing mystery. I mean, get this, the missing people are for the most part unrelated, yet they were all reported missing at about the same time some seven years ago."

"Unrelated?" Wade questioned. "The missing people are unrelated? What's that got to do with anything? How many people are missing?"

Parker explained, "Well, I don't know much about it yet, but I have learned that there's apparently no connection between all those missing people—well, maybe a few of them—but they weren't all coworkers, friends, relatives, so why did they all go missing at the same time? Where were they, why were they there, what in the heck happened to them, and how did their belongings end up in that cat colony?"

"Wrong place at the wrong time, I guess," Wade said. He added, "Hey, that assignment sounds like it's right up your alley, Sis. Congratulations."

"Thanks," Parker said a little hesitantly.

Wade frowned. "Why the reticence? Where's that Parker confidence?"

"Oh, I guess I'm always a little reticent when I embark on a new assignment or case." She tilted her head. "Reticent? Where are you getting these words? I never hear you use words like that."

Wade grinned, then asked, "How are the Iveys? You sure surprised me when you texted that you were at their house. You went there to stop a group of protestors at a cat expo?"

She nodded. "Yes, and I've been asked to write an article about that fiasco. Wade, you should have seen Savannah's cat, Rags, in action. Wow! Anyway," she said, "the Iveys are wonderful. Yeah, they were sure surprised to find out you're my brother."

"What a coincidence," Wade said.

"Who are these people?" Elaine asked.

"Michael and Savannah Ivey are friends of Brett Clampton," Wade said. "You know, the owner of the ranch where I'm working now in Colorado. They're both veterinarians. Michael runs a veterinary clinic, so he has business savvy, and Savannah has had experience managing horses, so Brett invited them out to Colorado to help him establish his dude ranch business."

"They're both veterinarians?" Elaine asked.

Parker nodded. "But Savannah's on leave while raising their two adorable children. She also manages one of the most unique cats I've ever known."

"Which is actually how I met them," Wade said. "It was because of the cat that I landed the job at the Lady B Ranch."

"You met them through Rags?" Parker asked. "I haven't heard that story."

"Rags?" Elaine repeated, frowning.

"That's Savannah's cat, Ragsdale," Parker explained. She faced Wade. "So they helped you get that job?"

"Yes," Wade said. "Savannah was walking around town with Rags, and this old guy thought the cat was a stray. I guess he didn't see the leash. So he decides to grab the cat and take him home. Well, when he realizes the cat's on a leash and that Savannah's still holding the other end of it, he starts running. Savannah isn't about to let go, and I guess neither was he. When I saw what was going on, I tackled the guy. By then Savannah had dropped the leash—well, she fell—and the cat got away from her. So here I am trying to wrestle the cat from that old guy's grip when Michael and his twin brother show up and they get involved. The guy finally turns loose, and Rags runs back to Savannah none the worse for wear."

"That's how you met them?" Parker asked. "That's crazy."

"That cat's crazy," Wade said.

"It doesn't sound to me like the cat did anything wrong," Elaine said. "Talk about the wrong place at the wrong time."

Wade chuckled. "That's a specialty of Rags's."

"He's actually quite an awesome cat," Parker said. "He works with a detective in the town where they live up north."

"Doing what?" Elaine asked skeptically.

"Helping solve crimes," Parker said.

"Like Olivia does?" Elaine asked, petting the cat that lay next to her in a cushy corduroy chair.

Parker nodded. "Except that he's a klepto cat." She jumped a little in her seat. "I brought you some books about him. I think you'll enjoy them." She giggled. "Savannah calls them Rags's meowmoirs. Meowmoirs, get it?"

"Oh?" Elaine said. "Sounds interesting. Where are they?"

"I'll give them to you tomorrow," Parker said. "They're for Christmas." She asked her brother, "So Way-Way, how's it going in Colorado?"

"Great!" Wade said. "I really like the people, especially Brett. He's about my age. He went to college planning to land a job in the finance field, but he was drawn to the out-of-doors. He started hiking the trails in Colorado and eventually began giving tours. One thing led to another, and he left the numbers world and bought the ranch. He's running it as a dude ranch. I'm the main wrangler, but I get to do other things too. Right now, I'm helping rehabilitate a mountain lion."

"What?" Elaine squealed.

Wade nodded. "Yeah, I'm working with the local zoo veterinarian." He chuckled. "Jason's a top-notch vet, but he doesn't have a great bedside manner, so I volunteered to be a sort of advocate for the mountain lion—you know, interpret for him."

"Amazing," Elaine said. She glanced at Parker. "Both of you. You're not exactly doing what I would have imagined for you, but you're happy, you're making a difference, and you're following your passion. What more could a mother want?" She grinned and said emphatically, "Except grandchildren."

Wade winked at his mother, then tilted his head and asked, "Is someone at the door?"

"Son," Elaine said, "are you doing that psychic stuff again? I thought you only did it with animals." She looked suspiciously at him. "Or are we being visited by a local sea lion or…"

"Maybe it's Alejandro," Parker said, "coming to see Olivia."

"Who?" Wade asked.

"Donny's and Cecilia's cat."

He chuckled and walked swiftly to the door. When he returned he was not alone. A woman who appeared to be in her thirties accompanied him.

Elaine took one look at her and gasped. "Oh my God!" She stood up, took hold of the woman's arm, and hissed, "Pamela, I told you not to come here this week."

The woman pulled back and spat, "What's the matter, are you ashamed of me?"

"Please, this is not the time or the place," Elaine said.

"Yeah?" the stranger snarked. "When, Elaine? When do you suggest I return—never?"

"What is it, Mom?" Wade asked. He looked more closely at the woman. "I have the feeling I should know you. You look familiar." He glanced from the woman to his mother expecting an answer.

"I *should* look familiar," the woman said.

"Pamela, no," Elaine warned, attempting to lead her toward the front door. More quietly she said, "I told you I'd call you after I've talked to them."

Pamela pulled loose, faced Elaine, and grasped her upper arms. When Elaine tried to turn away Pamela said, "Can't you even look at me? Look at me!" she shouted. "Don't you think it's time you come clean? Can't you see it's wrong to keep us apart?" She blinked back tears. "It's Christmas Eve. I refuse to spend another Christmas alone crying myself to sleep, when I have a family. I want to know my family."

Parker moved closer and demanded, "What's going on?" She stood shoulder-to-shoulder with her mother and asked the stranger, "Who are you? Why are you talking to my mother like this?"

Pamela stepped back and asked, "Are you going to tell them, Elaine, or shall I?"

When Elaine turned away, Pamela slumped and huffed a couple of times, then she lifted the bottom of her wide-legged slacks to reveal what appeared to be a birthmark on her calf. She asked, "Does this ring any bells, Parker?"

"You know me?" Parker asked, squinting suspiciously at her. "How? Who are you?" She thought for a moment, then pointed at Pamela's leg. "Wait, I've seen that before. It looks like a cat. It's shaped like a cat. Yes, I remember it." She studied Pamela. "But I don't remember you. Who are you?"

Pamela smiled. "So you do remember my birthmark. You used to touch it and say, 'kitty-kitty.'" She laughed. "You loved cats. All of your picture books had cats in them, and you played with toy cats all the time. Your favorite cat was a stuffed calico your grandfather found in a thrift store. Do you remember that?"

"You lived with us," Parker said in a near whisper. "Oh my gosh, I haven't thought about that in years. You're Melly. Is that right? Are you Melly?"

"You lived with us?" Wade asked.

"That was before you were born, right, Mom?" Parker asked. "Melly lived with you and me and Dad until I was four or five years old, didn't she?" She looked at Pamela. "Where did you go? I woke up one day and you were gone. I missed you so much it hurt."

Pamela nodded. "Yes, I was eight when it happened."

"What?" Parker asked. "What happened?"

"Why don't we all sit down?" Wade suggested. "Would that be okay, Mom?"

Elaine let out a sigh of defeat. "I guess." She lowered herself into the corduroy chair and watched as the others found their area of comfort. Parker motioned for Pamela to sit on the sofa, then she sat down. Olivia jumped up between them. The cat looked Pamela over, then stretched out and lay next to Parker.

Wade perched on a chair in the middle of the three women, resting his elbows on his knees. "Who are you?" he asked. "Why did you live with our family? Why haven't I ever met you? Or have we met before?" He shook his head. "You do look familiar."

Rather than respond, Pamela lashed out at Elaine. "You were expecting him when you sent me away. You could take care of another baby, but you couldn't take care of me. I also want to know why? Why, Elaine? No one has ever given me a clear answer. Will you answer Parker and Wade—the children you kept? Why did I get kicked to the curb, and they got to stay?"

Elaine took a ragged breath. "Pamela, it wasn't my decision or my choice. You have to believe that."

"Mom," Parker pleaded, "what's this about?"

"It seems that this family has a secret, Sis," Wade said. "Mom, why won't you answer this woman? It appears that Parker and I need answers as well, to questions we didn't even know existed."

Elaine stood up and turned away.

"Mom?" Parker said. When there was no response she asked Pamela. "Who are you? What happened back then?"

Before either Pamela or Elaine could speak, there was another knock at the door. Wade stood up, walked to the door, and opened it.

"Watch Olivia!" Parker shouted when she saw the cat trotting after Wade.

He stepped outside and closed the door behind him, returning minutes later. He gazed around the room at the others. Parker still sat on the sofa with Pamela, Elaine slouched in her chair, and Olivia sat on the coffee table watching Wade. Everyone chuckled when the cat leaped into his chair ahead of him and sat down as if she belonged there.

"Patches," he said. "What do you think you're doing?" He picked her up and sat down with her on his lap, but she quickly jumped to the floor and ran at full speed into the hallway, chirping in her squeaky, high-pitched voice."

"Did you just insult my cat?" Parker teased.

He raised his eyebrows. "I guess I did."

"Who was it, Son?" Elaine asked without emotion.

"Your neighbor," he said. "She wanted to thank us for helping them with that little boy today—Cecilia's her name, right?" Elaine nodded, and he continued, "She said they're keeping the tyke in the hospital at least overnight, and they have Child Protective Services involved."

"Good," Parker cheered. "There was something wrong with that woman—his mother." She grinned wickedly. "I wonder if she made her dinner date."

Ignoring her, Wade looked around at the others and asked, "So do we know anything more about Melly—why she lived with our family, and why she was sent away? I'd sure like to know what that was about."

"All I know," Pamela said, "is that I was a happy child. I felt like I belonged, until I was sent away." She faced Elaine. "Do you know what that does to a kid? It pretty much ruined my life, knowing that I wasn't wanted—that I had been discarded like some of those cats Parker used to drag home. Do you know how much that hurt—how much damage that did to me?"

"Pamela," Elaine said, sitting forward in her chair. She spoke more assertively, "I'm sorry, but that was a long time ago. Can't you forget the past and concentrate on making a life for yourself?"

"You just don't get it, do you, Elaine?" Pamela spat. "My life is crap. I've spent years in therapy trying to repair whatever self-esteem I had left. Every relationship I've ever been in has done more damage. Because of you and your selfishness, I'll never be okay. I know that now; I'll never be okay."

"Mom," Parker said, "what happened? Why did Melly have to go away?" More quietly, she asked, "Is Melly our sister?"

Elaine looked at Parker and started to weep. Everyone watched and waited for her to speak. Finally, she looked up to the heavens and said, "God, forgive me." She took a ragged breath, and looked into Pamela's face. "It wasn't me, Pamela; it was your father."

"Daddy?" Pamela said, her voice weak. "Daddy sent me away?"

"No, dear. You see, the daddy you knew is not your father, and I'm not your mother."

"What?" Pamela shouted. "But…"

Just then a clatter and crash interrupted the conversation.

"I'll check," Wade said, taking long strides into the hallway. He returned with Olivia in his arms. "She just knocked over a picture, that's all."

"A picture?" Elaine questioned.

"One of those you have sitting on that hallway table," he explained, dropping Olivia onto Parker's lap.

Olivia scurried up onto the back of the sofa, lay down, and stared at Pamela.

Elaine took advantage of the silence and said, "Listen, Pamela, I'm only going to say this once. I agree that you should have been told. I just hoped someone else would do the telling, like your father. He didn't explain anything to you?"

"What do you mean?" Pamela shrieked. She covered her face with her hands. "My God, who are my parents? Who am I? Are you saying that man you sent me away with when I was eight years old is my father? He sure didn't act like it."

Elaine felt like she'd been kicked in the stomach. She wiped tears from her cheeks, sat forward, and said, "Yes, he is your father. I'm sorry, and…"

When Pamela began to sob uncontrollably, Parker took her hand. "Come sit closer to me. Let's find out the truth together, shall we, Melly?"

"You don't know?" Pamela asked. "Parker, you really don't know?"

Parker shook her head. She held tightly to Pamela's hand and said, "Go on, Mom."

Meanwhile, Olivia jumped down onto Parker's lap and wriggled into the space between the two women. Parker smiled down at Olivia, but the cat seemed more concerned about their guest. She looked up at Pamela, resting a paw on her thigh.

Pamela's pain was too raw, however, and she scarcely noticed.

Elaine dabbed at her eyes with a tissue, saying, "I was the oldest child in my family, and when…"

"Wait," Wade said, "I thought you were the *only* child."

Elaine nodded. "For most of my life, that's right, but I had two sisters. Karen died of leukemia as a child and Lori, who was a year younger than me, was killed in a motorcycle accident when she was eighteen years old."

"What does that have to do with me?" Pamela asked. "Oh, wait, are you saying…"

"Let Mom tell the story," Wade suggested.

Olivia mewed softly, and pressed her paw gently against Pamela's leg.

"Lori had just given birth to a beautiful baby girl out of wedlock," Elaine continued. "The father walked away as soon as he heard there was going to be a baby. He joined the military in order to avoid any responsibility for the child—for you, Pamela. When your mother died I took you in."

Pamela began to weep. "You're not my mother? You're my aunt?" she asked weakly.

Elaine nodded. "Yes. I dropped out of college in order to give you a home. My parents—your grandparents—helped. I carried the scorn of having a child out of wedlock, until Jerry Colton came along. He wanted to marry me even though I had a child. Pamela, you were my child—mine and Jerry's. We loved you as if you were our own."

"Then you had Parker and Wade and decided to give me away?" Pamela asked, weeping.

"No. That's not how it happened," Elaine insisted.

"Then what did happen?" Pamela asked. "Tell me!" she shouted.

Olivia looked up at Pamela and mewed softly.

"Your birth father came back," Elaine said quietly. She choked up. "He was discharged from the military. I'd heard that he'd also spent time in jail. The last thing he needed was a child, and the last thing you needed was him for a father. Well, I guess somehow he found out that Lori had died and that you were with us, and he came after you with a vengeance. Your daddy and I fought for you because we knew you were safer and would have a better life with us. We fought for you and we lost. We had no choice. The courts had spoken."

"Why didn't you come get me when things got bad?" Pamela asked. "You must have known things would be awful for me."

"Yes, I was pretty sure of that. That's what we were trying to protect you from, but after he took you, we had no idea where you were. Your father cut off all contact," Elaine explained.

Pamela sniffled. "I don't have much memory of that time in my life or of him. I think he was tall. I remember him having a moustache and bushy eyebrows."

Elaine nodded. "Yes, well, from what I found out later, he went to prison again, this time for many years, and he turned you over to another family to raise. But it was all rumors—word of mouth—and we still couldn't find out where you were."

"In a small town in Arkansas," Pamela spat, "with the cockroaches."

"What?" Wade said.

"Oh, their name was Conkright or Cronkite or something. They were awful." Pamela looked at Elaine. "I prayed every day you'd come get me, but you never came." She shook her head slowly. "You never came. I thought you didn't want me. I went out on my own as soon as I was legally able. Oh, I ran away numbers of times. I was quite familiar with juvie. In fact, that became kind of my safe place, but I'd always end up back at the cockroaches." She took a ragged breath. "It wasn't until I was eighteen that I could legally break out on my own and I did, but that didn't go well, either." She raised her hands for effect. "Looking back, what would you expect from someone who had very little upbringing. Food on the table—*check*; clothes to wear in public—*check*; but other than that, nothing. No affection," she glanced around at the others, "at least not of the motherly or fatherly kind, and no parenting to speak of. I had a couple of teachers who helped me through some tough spots, and I always had memories of what a home should be like." She looked across the room at Elaine. "Your home, Elaine. My home with you, Mommy, and my Daddy, and baby sister, Parker."

Elaine blotted at her eyes, and Pamela continued, "When I realized I wasn't doing well on my own…" She grimaced. "I have to tell you, jail is a lot different than juvie. Well, I started thinking about things, and I decided that maybe if I could find you, Elaine—my first mother—if I could come full circle back to my beginnings, maybe I'd be able to repair my broken life."

Just then Olivia stepped onto Pamela's lap and looked up into her face. Pamela petted her a little awkwardly at first. Dubious, she asked, "What's she doing?"

Everyone smiled when Olivia flopped up against Pamela and lay down. "Oh," Pamela yelped. "Well, how nice. Isn't she sweet? She makes me feel so—you know, kind of special."

Parker smiled and ran her hand over Olivia's fur, saying, "That's a specialty of hers."

Pamela took a couple of deep breaths, then snuggled with the cat, murmuring, "Thank you, sweet kitty. Thank you." She looked around at the others. "Where was I?" she asked, sounding calmer now.

"You were talking about your broken life," Wade said.

Pamela looked at him, then at Parker, and said, "I found Elaine last week and told her I want to know the two of you. When she refused to give me your contact information, I felt even more abandoned, as you can imagine."

"But you found us, didn't you?" Wade said.

Pamela grinned. "Yes, I watched the house. I figured since it's Christmas week, maybe you'd come around, or that Elaine would lead me to you."

"You've been watching my house?" Elaine asked. "Why would you do that?"

"I want to know my family," Pamela insisted. "Is that so unusual? Is there something wrong with that?"

"Well, Pamela, you never knew Wade at all, and Parker was so young—you had no real memories together. You grew up in such different environments. What could you possibly have in common with her?"

"What does that have to do with anything?" Pamela insisted. "I'd like to get to know my siblings—or, I guess they're my cousins. They're my blood cousins, right?"

Wade stared at Pamela for a moment, then he walked into the hallway, returning with a photograph. "This is the picture Olivia knocked down a while ago. It just dawned on me why you look familiar, Pamela." He showed it to Elaine. "This is a picture of one of our aunts, right, Mom? Is this Pamela's mother?"

Elaine nodded.

"I want to see it," Pamela insisted. "Let me see." She took the picture from Wade. "Oh my gosh. Why didn't you show this to me before, Elaine? I do look like her, don't I?" She gazed at Elaine. "But so do you." She glanced at the others. "I actually look like I belong in this family."

"Yes, you do, Pamela," Elaine said.

She gazed at Elaine. "I think I remember a grandmother who looked a lot like you do now. I hope I have that pretty salt-and-pepper hair when I'm your age." She frowned. "I still don't understand why you sent me away. You said you wanted me and that you looked for me, but when I came here last week you sent me away again. Why?"

Parker faced her mother. "Mom, I have to wonder that, too. Why did you push Pamela away? I've never known you to be callous like that. You raised her until she was eight years old. How could you...?"

Elaine began to choke up. "It wasn't like that." It took her a few moments to regain her composure, then she said, "I can't tell you how much it hurt to have you snatched from me, Pamela. It was the worst time in my life. It was like someone tore you from my heart, and there was absolutely nothing I could do to get you back. I tried, Pamela. Believe me, we tried, but I had to let you go. I had absolutely no legal rights to you. Once the reality set in, once I knew you were gone and I would never hold you, or braid your hair, or read a book with you again, I had a lot of work to do in order to heal. In fact, I was close to having a breakdown. Here I was with a wonderful little daughter and about to have a baby, yet I was experiencing some of my darkest days."

"But think of me," Pamela said, leaning forward. She watched as Olivia jumped down off her lap, then she continued, "You lost one child. I lost everything."

Wade put up his hand. "You had the opportunity to talk about your feelings, Pamela. You asked why Mom did what she did. How about giving her a chance to speak? Can't you see she's hurting, too?"

Pamela sat back in her seat and crossed her arms over her chest.

When Elaine seemed at a loss for words, Parker prompted, "You said you had a lot of work to do in order to heal. How did you go about that, Mom? It sounds like it was quite daunting."

Elaine nodded. "I'm not sure the hole in my heart ever healed, but I eventually found a way to go on with my life. I had to let you go, Pamela, and trust that you'd be okay. It was that simple and that complicated." She took a few moments to calm herself, then said, "When you showed up last week, well, that opened the wound again and it started bleeding. I couldn't…I just couldn't open my arms to you. It meant reliving all the pain, and Pamela, I just didn't have it in me. I'm so sorry. I must have seemed horribly callous, as Parker said. I didn't even stop to think about what you've gone through, and how much it would mean to you to be part of a family—your real family. All I could think about was my pain and how your presence had started the nightmare all over again. I'm sorry," she said, standing up. She opened her arms. "Pamela, can you ever forgive me?"

The two women held each other and cried for several moments, then Parker took a ragged breath, and she hugged them both at the same time. It didn't take long for Wade to join in. He wrapped his arms around the three women.

Elaine was first to pull back. She took Pamela's face in her hands and said, "Welcome home, Melly." She kissed Pamela on the cheek, then patted Parker's face and Wade's. "Thank you all for helping me to see my way clear. We'll all heal together, how about that?"

Parker grabbed her cousin and hugged her tightly. "Welcome back, Melly. Oh, this is so exciting!" She turned to her brother. "Wade, Pamela is our only real cousin, do you know that? The others are all sorts of stepcousins and once- or twice-removed cousins, right, Mom?" She didn't wait for an answer. She just hugged Pamela again.

Pamela smiled from ear to ear while also wiping tears from her cheeks.

"Okay," Wade said, "this is all hunky-dory, but can we eat while we're healing?"

"Dinner!" Elaine exclaimed. "I forgot about dinner! Do we have reservations somewhere? Oh my gosh, I should have bought a ham or something. What in the world are we going to do for Christmas Eve dinner?"

"Shall I call out for pizza?" Parker suggested, grinning.

Pamela chuckled. "Yeah, how about turkey-and-stuffing pizza?"

Parker laughed out loud. "I'll have mine with cranberries."

"And peas," Wade said. "I've gotta have peas with my holiday meal."

Parker, trying to keep a straight face, asked, "Do you want pumpkin pie and whipped cream on that pizza?"

Suddenly the four of them were laughing so hard they could barely stand up straight. Parker threw herself on the sofa, next to where Olivia was sprawled, and tried to quell her laughter.

Wade doubled over, attempting to catch his breath between chortles. Pamela, too, was caught up in the hilarity.

"It wasn't that funny," Elaine said, trying to stifle her hysteria.

"It's not?" Parker asked, wiping at her eyes. She stood up and snatched a tissue from a box on the buffet across the room. "Then why can't I stop cackling?"

"You do cackle when you laugh," Pamela said, breaking out in uncontrollable laughter again.

Parker giggled. "At least I don't snort like you do."

"I snorted?" Pamela screeched. "Are you sure?" Seeing Parker wracked with giggles, she laughed even harder, then said, "Oops. I guess I did just snort." She dropped onto the sofa, causing Olivia to dive off onto the floor. Pamela tried to catch her breath, saying, "Oh my gosh, that was exhausting."

"Yeah," Wade said, "cracking up takes a lot out of you."

"I haven't had a workout like that since I ran that marathon last year," Parker admitted. She looked at her mother, who sat with her hand over her mouth, still attempting to control her remaining chuckles.

When they heard a loud meow, they all looked to see Olivia sitting on the dining room table tilting her head from side to side.

"Are we disturbing you?" Wade asked, picking up the cat and snuggling with her.

"She thinks we're all crazy," Pamela said. She frowned. "What was so funny, anyway?"

"Heck if I know," Wade said.

"Pizza!" Parker shouted. "I think it had to do with pizza." She grinned at Pamela. "And Melly's snorts."

Elaine stood up and waved a hand in the air. "Oh, stop it, you guys. Let's don't get started again." She struggled to curtail her urge to laugh, then said, "Parker, your cat's probably hungry and so am I. Now, where shall we go for dinner?"

"You want to take Olivia out to dinner?" Wade asked. Before anyone could respond, he suggested, "How about we dine in?"

"Okay," Elaine said. "I make a pretty good tuna salad sandwich, and we have cookies, brownies, and the yummiest pecan pie…"

Wade handed the cat to Parker, muttering, "Never mind, I've got dinner covered."

"You do?" Elaine asked.

The others waited for his response.

Wade glanced out a window. "Well, I sort of ordered a meal. It should be delivered just about any time." He pulled his phone from his pocket, looked at the screen, and said, "I'd better check to find out where it is."

Elaine put a hand on his arm. "It's not that awful-sounding pizza you kids were talking about is it?"

Wade grinned, put his phone to his ear, and walked into the kitchen. "It's here," he announced, returning. He opened the front door. "Dad," he greeted enthusiastically. "Mama-Gail," he said, hugging his stepmother affectionately.

"Well, I should have known," Elaine said, walking toward the couple. "I forgot you said you might make an appearance. Gail, it's so nice to see you," she said, hugging her. She pulled back and asked, "What's in the bag?"

Gail smiled. "Bakery pies and homemade cranberries."

Elaine raised her eyebrows in delight, then said, "Jerry, you're loaded down. What do you have there?"

"The rest of Christmas dinner," he said.

"Oh, this is wonderful," Elaine cheered. She motioned to them. "Come on, bring it into the kitchen; you'll need your arms free for hugging. I know you'll want to catch up with your children." More mysteriously, she added, "And we have a special surprise for you."

"A present?" Jerry asked, carefully distributing baking dishes and bowls over the kitchen counter.

Gail removed the pies from the bag and put one of them in the refrigerator, saying, "Coconut cream, for Parker."

"Merry Christmas, Elaine," her former husband said, pulling her to him for a brief hug.

"Merry Christmas to you both," Elaine said. "And thank you for taking over with the meal."

"Well, you're providing the venue," Jerry said. "It's the least we could do."

The trio returned to the living room where the chatter was lively, and Parker rushed into her father's arms. "I've missed you, Daddy. You look great."

"I feel great," he said, hugging her tightly. He pulled back. "Gail takes good care of me." He put one hand on his back and winced. "I still have that arthritis creeping up on me. My leg still aches sometimes where that dang colt nailed me, but other than that—yeah, I'm good."

Parker smiled. "I can see that." She embraced her stepmother. "You look great too, Gail."

"That's 'cause we're happy," Jerry said. "You must be happy, too. You look wonderful." He glanced around. "Hey, where's Patches?"

"Her name's Olivia," Gail corrected.

"Yes," Parker said. "Mom-Gail knows her grandcat's name."

Gail frowned. "Where is she?"

Pamela pointed into the kitchen. "On the counter with the food."

"Oh no. Olivia!" Parker called, trotting into the kitchen. "What happened to your manners?"

"I just saw her toss them out the window," Wade said, laughing. He gave his father a man hug. "Good to see you, Dad." He pulled back, wrapped one arm around Gail and kissed the side of her head. "I've missed you, Mama-Gail."

When Parker returned with Olivia, Jerry took the wriggling cat into his arms and ran a hand over her a couple of times. She immediately relaxed.

Parker chuckled. "You know her pressure points, don't you, Dad?"

"Gotta know those pressure points," he said. "How else can you expect to manage a cat?" He grinned. "So what trouble has she been in lately?"

Before Parker could respond, she saw Pamela moving closer. She stepped back and invited her to join them. "Dad, Gail," she said, "this is…"

"Pamela?" Jerry said inquisitively. He reached out with one hand. "Are you Pamela?"

She took his hand and nodded.

Jerry stood stunned for a moment, then muttered, "You're just as I imagined you'd be—a nice blend between Parker and Elaine." He shifted Olivia to one arm and pulled Pamela into a hug with the other, asking, "Where have you been, girl? I've missed you. Did that father of yours take good care of you like he promised he would?"

Pamela winced and lied, "Yeah, he did okay. I've sure missed you, though."

Jerry lowered Olivia onto the sofa, hugged Pamela again, then pulled back. "Gail, this is Pamela. I've told you about her."

"Yes!" Gail said. "Oh my, it's wonderful to meet you. Your dad has wondered where you were. He speaks of you often. Do you live around here?"

"He has?" Pamela asked. She looked at Jerry. "You talk about me?"

"Absolutely," he said. "We always hoped you'd come back to us."

"And she has," Elaine said, moving closer. "She finally has."

Jerry hugged Pamela again and murmured, "What a Christmas blessing." He glanced around the room. "We have all of our children together again." He pulled Gail to him. "Isn't it a blessing?"

Pamela wiped at her eyes. "And you've made this my best Christmas ever." She grinned. "Except for maybe the year we went on that sled ride in the snow when we visited those relatives in Connecticut." She asked, "Do you remember that, Mom?" She stuttered, "I…I mean Elaine."

Elaine nodded. "I sure do remember that. We had our first snowball fight, didn't we?" She looped arms with Pamela and Parker and nodded toward Gail. "Shall we put the food out? What do you think, buffet style?"

It didn't take long for the women to set the table and arrange the food platters. Then Elaine called, "Grab a plate and get in line." Everyone complied, except for Jerry, who cradled Olivia in his arms. Elaine petted Olivia and said, "Plate, Jerry, not cat." She then asked him, "Would you like to say a few words?"

"Is that the new turkey-carving ritual?" Jerry asked.

"Turkey-carving ritual?" Elaine repeated. She then said, "Oh, yes, I guess it is." When the younger people appeared confused, she explained, "When we were children..."

"In the olden days?" Wade teased.

"Yes," Elaine said. "Well, the man of the house sat at the head of the table on Christmas or Thanksgiving, and he carved the turkey in front of all the guests. In this case, the turkey is sliced, so..."

"Well, I'd be honored to speak," Jerry said, kissing Olivia's furry cheek and lowering her to the floor. He reached into his pocket and pulled out a sheet of paper, looked at it, and said, "Naw, that one's outdated. I'll have to wing it."

Gail smiled at her husband.

"Lord," he started, "I thought we were blessed to the hilt before I arrived here tonight. I want to thank you for this delicious meal we're about to receive." He chuckled. "And I know it's delicious because I taste-tested everything." He glanced around the room. "Thank you for this opportunity to spend time with my amazing children: Parker, my inquisitive, get-it-done daughter and Wade, my free-spirit and spirited son—both of whom we're awfully proud, mostly because they're happy and they're making a difference. We love you both." He looked down at Olivia, who was standing up with her paws against his leg. He picked her up again and cuddled her. "Yes, Olivia, I love you too."

"What about my horses and my dog and..." Wade said.

Parker gave Wade a playful nudge. "You don't even own an animal now."

Jerry grinned at her, then continued, "Elaine, this family is blessed by your generosity and grace. Gail and I want you to know how much we appreciate your open door and your open heart. I love that we've remained family through all of these years. And I want to mention Greg Campbell. We've missed his presence these past two years. I couldn't have chosen a better stepfather for our children."

Elaine smiled and fought back tears.

Jerry turned toward Pamela. "I had to discard my original speech today because of you, Melly. Elaine will tell you that you have always been included in our Christmas blessing." When he noticed Parker and Wade looking at him quizzically, he said, "Yeah, I doubt you kids knew the meaning of it, but it was meaningful to your mom and me. Usually, Pamela, I would say something like…" he dug out the paper and read, "'…and blessings to those we love and cherish, but who, for one reason or another, cannot be here today.'" He choked up. "And here you are. So today I can say, Thank you Lord for bringing Pamela home. May she never lose her way to our homes and our hearts."

Pamela moved forward, wrapped her arms around him, and wept. She pulled back. "You can bet on it…um, Uncle Jerry."

"So you've been told the story of your birth, have you?" Jerry asked.

Pamela nodded.

"You know you used to call me *Daddy*."

"I remember," she said.

"If it's okay with you—I mean if you want to—you can still call me *Daddy*."

"Thanks, Daddy." She looked at Elaine. "Would you believe, I've never called anyone mom or dad since I lived here? Do you think it would be okay…would you mind if I…?"

Elaine nodded. "I'd love to be your mom again."

"What's that?" Wade asked, looking around.

"What?" a couple of others asked.

"It sounds almost like a growl."

Parker nodded toward Olivia, who was now in Gail's arms. "She's purring."

"Mom-Gail is purring?" Wade asked.

Parker laughed. "No, Olivia is. She has those squeaky soprano mews, but a baritone purr. Deep, isn't it?"

Wade shook his head. "That cat is so weird, aren't you, Patches?"

"Shall I just put her down here on the floor?" Gail asked.

"Mom?" Parker said, taking Olivia from Gail.

"Yes," Elaine said, "I set her a place."

When Pamela looked at Wade he rolled his eyes. "Yeah, the cat's spoiled, what can I say? Someone's gotta get Mom some grandkids."

Pamela laughed. "Well, don't look at me."

Once everyone, including Princess Olivia, was seated around the table, Parker asked, "Hey, Mom, where's your tree? I just noticed you didn't put one up this year. I brought you a present. Where will I put it?"

Elaine smiled at her, then at the others. "I can't imagine getting a better gift than the one you all gave me this evening."

"Do you mean bringing Melly back into the family?" Parker asked.

"Yes, having all of my children with me—all of us together."

When they heard the doorbell, everyone looked around at one another. Wade said, "Who could that possibly be? We're all here and accounted for." He stood up and walked toward the front door.

At the same time, Parker grabbed Olivia just before she jumped down from her chair. "Where do you think you're going, sweet girl?"

"Maybe it's someone calling on her," Jerry joked.

Elaine chuckled. "Yeah, Alejandro."

"Who?" Gail asked curiously.

"The cat next door. He's a beautiful Maine coon tabby, and he was absolutely infatuated with Olivia the last time she was here."

"Parker," Wade said, interrupting.

She looked up and saw a policeman standing behind him. "What?" she asked.

Wade hesitated, then said, "He wants to talk to you about your cat."

Parker stood up, glanced around at the others, and walked toward the pair.

Wade led them into the living room out of earshot of the others, and the officer asked, "Parker Campbell?"

She nodded.

"I'm Sergeant Sheffield. I understand it was your cat that was with the boy, Oliver, when he was found this afternoon."

"Yes," Parker said. "She found him and stayed with him until help came and he could be removed from under the house." When she realized that Olivia was standing at her feet growling, she picked her up. "What is it, Olivia?"

"That's a pretty cat," the sergeant said.

"Yes, she is," Parker agreed. She smiled. "Does the police department want to give her a citation?"

"A what?" he asked.

"For saving the boy," Parker explained. When the sergeant winced, his eyes avoiding hers, she suddenly felt awash with dread. "Well, what is it you want to know," she asked. "We're in the middle of Christmas dinner."

"Sorry about that. It couldn't be helped." The sergeant looked at Olivia. "She's a pretty cat, but she doesn't sound very friendly there."

Parker attempted to calm Olivia, but the cat continued to growl.

"The thing is, ma'am, the boy's mother wants to have the cat examined."

"Examined?" Parker asked, glancing at Wade for his reaction.

"It appears, Ms. Campbell, that the cat may have bitten and scratched the boy, and the mother wants her checked over by a veterinarian. I'm afraid she's screaming about a lawsuit and maybe an order to have the cat put down."

"What?" Parker screeched, holding more tightly to Olivia.

Wade moved closer to Parker. "Now wait just a minute. Like my sister said, Olivia found the boy and sat with him until the police could get him out from under the house."

"Yeah," the sergeant said, "but a complaint's been filed and we have an obligation to honor it. I have a carrier out there on the porch, and I need to take her with me. By the way, do you have her health records with you?"

"No," Parker said, realizing her voice was an octave higher than usual. "Of course not. Not with me. I wasn't planning to cross any state lines or take a flight or... my veterinarian has them, but he's not open on Christmas Eve. What do you mean, you have to take her? Please, can't I just bring her to the station tomorrow or the next day? She's not used to being away from me. You see, we travel together and..."

As if he hadn't heard her, he asked, "Has she had her rabies vaccine and all those other vaccines cats need?"

Parker nodded. "Of course. Like I said, I travel with her. She's had all of her shots. She's a therapy cat and goes into nursing homes and hospitals."

"Really?" he said. "But you can't prove any of this?"

"On Christmas Eve?" she screeched. "No."

"Well, it doesn't sound like there'll be a problem, but I still have to take her until the examination is complete and the right paperwork reaches our office," he explained.

"No!" Parker protested.

The officer stepped outside and retrieved the carrier. "You can put her in there if you would."

"But officer," she wailed.

"I'm sorry, ma'am. Just doing my job."

When Wade saw that his sister couldn't bear to comply with the officer's wishes he gently took Olivia from her and closed the cat in the carrier. "Where will she be?" Wade asked.

"We have your number. We'll be in touch," the sergeant said.

"No!" Parker shouted. She tried to run after the officer, but Wade held her back. Solemnly, they watched as Olivia was carried away.

Chapter Three

"My God, Wade," Parker cried, "what just happened?"

"Nothing that can't be cleared up in a day or two," he soothed. "I'll stay here with you until we get her back. It'll be okay."

"Okay?" she said. "Wade, she's an escape artist—a Houdini. It takes a lot of MacGyvering to keep her confined." Parker ran to the door and pulled it open. "I should have told him that." When she saw the police car pull away she shouted, "No! Wait! Damn!" she said, stomping her foot. "Ouch!"

"Come on, Parker," Wade said, guiding her back into the house.

"I think I broke my foot," she complained, hopping after him on one foot.

"Well, if you'd calm down and stop beating yourself up..." he started.

"What's going on?" Jerry asked, entering the living room.

"They took Olivia," Wade said.

"Who, for God's sake?" Jerry asked. "That police officer?"

Parker lowered herself to the sofa and huffed, "Yes, and that's wrong! Just wrong. Wrong! What does that woman think she's doing, launching a complaint against poor Olivia?"

"For what?" Jerry asked. "What did she do?"

"Nothing," Parker said emphatically.

When Wade saw the others looking anxiously at them from the dining room table he said, "Hey, let's go finish our Christmas dinner, shall we? Come on, Dad," he urged. "We'll tell you all about it." When Parker remained seated on the sofa rubbing her foot he asked, "Are you all right?"

"Yeah," she said, standing up. She limped a little as she walked with him back into the dining room.

Wade put his arm around her and whispered, "It'll be okay." He then said, "Come on, let's relax and enjoy our delicious Christmas dinner, shall we? Then we'll figure some strategy."

Later that night after Jerry and Gail had left, Parker retired to her bedroom, leaving her mother, brother, and newly discovered cousin to chat. After a short time Parker returned. "Excuse me for interrupting."

Elaine reached for her daughter's hand. "Oh honey, I thought you'd gone to bed. Can't you sleep?" She took a second look. "You're dressed. Are you going out? What, for a walk or something?"

Parker shook her head and asserted, "No. I'm going to go get my cat." She faced her brother. "Wade, come on. You're going to help me get her back."

"I am?" he asked apprehensively. "Just how do you expect to do that? Do you even know where she is?"

"Yes. I called the nearest precinct and got in touch with Officer Spencer. Remember, he was here this afternoon. He gave me some information, and I want to follow up on it, like tonight—now."

Wade seemed to be thinking for a moment. Soon he let out a breath and said, "Par-Par, I believe she's okay. I'm not getting that she's terribly stressed. I think you should wait at least until morning."

Parker stomped her foot again. "Dammit, Wade..."

He chuckled a little nervously. "You'd better stop doing that. You really are going to hurt yourself."

In response, she picked up Wade's jacket and tossed it to him.

"Parker," he complained, "don't you trust my instincts anymore?"

"Come on," she insisted. "You know you don't get much clarity when you do telepathy at a distance."

Wade grinned at her, and Pamela asked, "How would you know what's going on with the cat, Wade? Or are you just doing that guy thing where anytime a woman's upset about something, you say stupid things like, 'No one will take your purse,' or 'She won't die,' or 'That dog's not going to bite you.'"

Parker laughed. "Men do that, don't they?"

"Yes," Pamela said. She pushed up one sleeve and exposed a scar on her arm, saying, "By the way, the dog *did* bite. Not only did I have to go through rabies treatment, I was tossed in jail for defacing government property." She grinned. "Yeah, that guy also said, 'Come on, Pamela. We won't get caught.'"

Parker thought for a moment about what her cousin had said, then explained, "Wade does have a way of communicating with animals." She asked, "So, Way-Way, do you think you actually talked to her? Is she really okay?"

He winced. "I tried, but her mind is a hard one to crack. She's kind of all over the place. I couldn't get her to focus."

Parker sighed. "Knowing Olivia, she's fighting this thing as hard as she can, and she isn't paying any attention to you."

He nodded. "I think you're right." He stood up and put on his jacket. "So where are we going?"

"I have the address here. It's not far."

"Do you have her harness?" he asked.

Parker nodded. She hugged her mother. "Wish us luck,"

"I do, honey. Be careful," Elaine said.

Parker hugged Pamela. "It was nice getting to spend time with you. I'm so sorry this happened. Maybe we can get together again before I leave for San Francisco."

"Most likely," Pamela said. She smiled. "I've been invited to stay."

"Oh, that's right," Parker said. "Over dinner you said you had your belongings in your car."

Elaine stood up. "Well, let me help you bring your things in, Pamela, and I'll show you to your room."

"Thank you." Pamela slipped into her jacket and waved to her cousins. "Good luck, you guys."

"So she's at the precinct?" Wade asked as Parker drove out of her mother's neighborhood. "I thought they'd have someone from animal control pick her up."

"I believe that's the plan, but Officer Spencer said he'd make sure that doesn't happen before we get there."

"What can you say that you didn't say to that sergeant, Parker—you know, that will make a difference?" Wade asked.

"I can show her inoculation records for one thing, and her therapy-cat certificate," she said. "I'd forgotten that I'd put those on my phone to make it easier to travel with her. Everything's on my phone, these days. Isn't that how you do it? It sure saves having to carry documents and purses and tote bags."

He chuckled. "You always seem to have a purse and a tote bag and a litter box, anyway."

"But no documents," she said flippantly. She drove into the precinct parking lot. "Here we are. Let's go get my girl."

"Parker," Wade said, grabbing her arm, "I want you to stay calm. Do you think you can do that? Nothing can be accomplished by you losing your cool. It's possible that they'll have to keep her overnight."

"Why are you saying that?" she demanded.

"I want you to be prepared just in case we can't bring her home. At least you'll know where she is, and that she's okay."

"Yeah, but I came here to bring her home," Parker insisted, scrambling out of the car. "Let's go get her."

Wade blew out a long breath as he exited the car. "Wait up," he called, trotting to catch up with her.

"Hello, I'm Parker Campbell. Is Officer Spencer here?" she asked as she approached the desk clerk.

"He just left on a call. May I help you?" the woman asked.

Parker slumped. She glanced around the

lobby. "Did he tell you I was coming to get my cat?"

"Cat?" she asked, frowning.

Impatiently, Parker explained, "A cop came to our house earlier this evening and took my cat on some bogus claim. I spoke with Officer Spencer a few minutes ago, and he said my cat's here. I want..."

Before she could complete her sentence, another woman entered the lobby. She smiled. "Oh, the pretty cat. Are you her owner?"

"Yes," Parker said, eagerly. "Do you know where she is? I came to take her home. She does not belong in a cage at a police station."

"What's she in here for, anyway?" the woman behind the desk asked. She glanced at the other woman, then at Parker and Wade.

"She apparently found a missing child this afternoon," the second woman explained. She offered her hand to Parker. "I'm Officer Inez Franklin. Officer Spencer told me you'd be coming in." She grinned. "He said the pretty girl's accused of assaulting the boy, but Spence doesn't believe it's true. Did he tell you that?"

"Neither do I," Parker said. "The only way she would have put any marks on the boy is in her exuberance to save him—you know, like if she tried to wake him up or drag him to safety. Olivia would never hurt a child. She locates and saves children."

"Olivia?" the officer repeated. "I've heard of a calico named Olivia." She looked at Parker and tilted her head. "Hey, are you Parker Campbell? Is that cat Olivia, the amazing calico that fights crime?"

"Well, I don't know about her fighting crime, but yes, I'm Parker Campbell. You know my work?"

The officer smiled. "Everyone around here knows your work." She frowned. "I can't believe Olivia has been detained."

"I guess anyone can make up lies and launch erroneous complaints against any innocent cat," Parker complained.

"Oh wait," Officer Franklin said, "the boy was Arianna Anderson's child, right?"

"Yes, I think that's her name," Parker said. "Can I please see Olivia? I'm really afraid for her."

Officer Franklin looked at Wade, who said, "My sister's a bit daft, you know. Do you think we could…"

She nodded. "I guess it would be okay. Spence said you have her inoculation records with you. That may be enough for us to release her." She turned away and said, "Just give me a few moments and we'll see what we can do."

"Oh please, yes," Parker said, excitedly. She watched the officer walk away, then looked at Wade. "Daft? Where are you getting these words?

What happened to your usual vocabulary, *buckaroo, dadgumit, yokel, yee-haw*?"

He chuckled. "I save that talk for my cowfolk friends. I have to step it up a notch when I'm hanging out with my sister, the famous journalist."

Parker grinned and shook her head.

"Why don't you let me take a look at those records," Officer Franklin said when she returned, "then we'll see about releasing the pretty girl." She was surprised when Parker pulled out her phone. "Oh, now that's a good idea." She scrolled through the information. "Looks to be in order." The officer explained, "I used to work with animal services. I think that's why Spence handed you over to me." She started to walk away, then turned back. "But I'll bet he didn't know you were Parker Campbell. This is cool." She turned toward the door. "Well come on, let's reunite you with Olivia." She added, "I love that name, and it really fits her—she's one gutsy, but beautiful, even maybe refined cat—at least according to how you represent her in some of your articles."

Parker and Wade exchanged looks, then followed Inez Franklin into a hallway. They walked past several rooms, stopping outside a door that was slightly ajar.

"They put her in the captain's office where it's quiet and no one will bother her. Come on," she said, leading the couple inside and switching on a light. She pointed. "She's right over here." The officer walked up to the carrier and blurted, "Oh no! She's not in there. Someone must have let her out. Who would have done that?"

"Did they already take her to animal services?" Wade asked.

"I doubt it," Officer Franklin said. "They would have taken the carrier."

"Let me look," Parker said, moving closer.

"I tell you, she's not in the cage," the officer confirmed.

"I know, but I want to see what kind of latch you have on there." After examining it, she announced, "Yeah, that's what I was afraid of. She let herself out."

"She broke out of jail?" Wade quipped.

"How?" the officer asked. "I've used that pen and others like it many times, and I've never had that happen." She hesitated, then said, "Well, maybe once. I do remember one guy, when I was working for animal services…" When she realized the others were more interested in finding Olivia than in hearing her story she said, "Okay, let's think about where she might go. Cats like to hide. Look under the desk there and behind the door. I'll check the closet. Could she be behind those books and things on that shelf?"

Wade moved books and bric-a-brac around on the shelf, then pointed. "That door was open when we came in. She could be anywhere in the building."

"Or she could have gone outside," Parker said, cringing at the thought. She stepped into the hallway and began calling for Olivia.

"Listen," Officer Franklin said, "I'm going to have to ask you to go back to the public area—you know, the lobby. We can't have people accessing these offices back here." When Parker hesitated she said, "Please, just go through that door at the end of the hall. I'll get a couple of staff members to help me look for Olivia. She can't have gone far."

"Come on, Sis," Wade said, taking her arm. "They'll find her."

"Damn, this infuriates me," Parker spat, once they were in the lobby. "I knew I should have stood tough and not allowed that man to take her."

"And get yourself arrested?" Wade said.

"Sure, then I could keep an eye on Olivia." She huffed and paced, finally saying, "I'm going out to look around." More excitedly she said, "Yeah, maybe she sneaked outside. She might have seen or heard us drive up, and she's waiting for me at the car. She knows the sound of my car."

"Okay," Wade said, "I'll go with you." He stopped and said to the desk clerk, "We'll be right out front in case you need us."

"Your cat escaped from custody?" the clerk asked. "We've never had that happen before." A few minutes later, when the couple returned, she said, "Doesn't look like you found her."

Parker shook her head and said to no one in particular, "Where in the heck could she be?" She faced the clerk. "We'd better find her, or this precinct will be in a world of hurt."

"Let's not get crazy," Wade cautioned. He then said, "Listen, I don't think she's in any danger. I really believe that. Now let's sit down and wait patiently for that Inez woman, shall we?"

Within minutes the inside door opened, and Officer Franklin entered the lobby.

"You didn't find her," Parker said. "I can tell by your posture."

"No, but there's one room I haven't looked in, yet," the officer said.

"A bathroom?" Parker asked. "Oh no, not a bathroom. She'll be playing in the toilet for sure. She likes water. In fact, she likes watching a toilet flush. Sometimes she even manages to flush it herself." She faced Wade. "I don't think I told you about our hotel stay in Mexico that time. We got in big trouble for wasting water while we were there. I couldn't for the life of me figure out why, then I caught Olivia sitting on the toilet seat just flushing and flushing away. She can also sometimes turn on a faucet."

"Oh my," the officer said, walking swiftly toward the door. "Come on, let's go see." She said over her shoulder, "I actually looked around in the women's restroom, but maybe we'd better check the men's." She stopped outside the bathroom door and motioned to Wade. "Sir, I'll let you go in." She asked Parker, "So Olivia likes water, does she?" She cringed. "You know, I heard some flushing going on in there when I was checking the women's facility. I figured that if she was in there, whoever was using the facility would see her."

"Well?" Parker asked eagerly when Wade returned.

"Officer Franklin," Wade said, "either you work with some squirrely officers, or someone turned loose a pack of monkeys in there." He shook his head. "It's a disaster—paper towels and toilet paper all over the place." He grinned at Parker. "I thought Olivia was more refined than that."

Parker sighed. "Not when she's unhappy or feels cornered. She'll take it out on whatever she can get her paws on."

When the officer heard a door open at the end of the hallway, she turned and called out, "Camille, can I speak with you for a moment?"

Camille nodded and said quietly as the trio approached, "I was just going to call you when I heard you out here." She glanced curiously at Parker and Wade.

"We're looking for a cat," Inez said. "Can we…"

"By all means," Camille said, cautiously opening the door for them to enter. She put her finger across her lips in a shushing manner and motioned for Inez to follow her across the room to a small futon covered with a blanket. Camille lifted a corner of the blanket, and Inez gasped. She eagerly motioned for the couple to join her.

Parker was sure her heart missed a beat as she approached the officer. When she got close enough, she could see an infant lying on the futon contentedly sucking her thumb. The baby held the edge of the blanket up against her face and stared out at Parker with wide eyes. The officer lifted another edge of the blanket and revealed a shock of black, orange, and white fur.

"Olivia!" Parker hissed. "Oh my gosh." She clasped her hands under her chin and smiled down at the baby and the cat.

"Is this your cat?" Camille asked. "What's she doing here at the station?"

"Long story," Wade said, running his hand over the sleeping calico.

Olivia raised her head and looked at him briefly through squinty eyes, then lay back down.

Parker cupped one hand over Olivia's head tenderly. "My sweet girl." She smiled down at her and at the baby.

"It's an abuse case," Camille explained. "We're waiting for social services. I guess maybe the cat heard the little thing crying in here. When I came in to relieve Wentzel, she must have sneaked in. I was freaked out when she suddenly appeared at my feet…"

Parker chuckled. "She does that. She seems to materialize out of thin air sometimes."

"So she just climbed into bed with the baby?" Inez asked, amused.

Camille nodded. "When I saw how gentle she was with the baby and how relaxed the little one became, well, it was the miracle we needed." She tilted her head. "Didn't I hear that a cat found the Anderson boy this afternoon?"

Parker nodded. "Yes, that was Olivia."

"That poor soul," Camille said. "He's another child who needs help."

Suddenly Olivia raised her head and looked around. She stood up, sniffed the child's face a couple of times, then stepped slowly onto the floor and stretched—her bushy tail arching across her back.

"Olivia, sweetheart," Parker cooed, kneeling. "Come here, girl. I missed you so much."

The pert calico stretched again, then walked up to Parker and put one paw on her leg. Everyone chuckled when Olivia reached up toward Parker's face with her other paw, waving it in the air a couple of times.

"What was that?" Wade asked.

Parker grinned and shook her head. "Heck if I know. She always does it. I assume it's a special greeting—she's greeting me."

"She missed you," Officer Franklin said, smiling.

"Yeah, we're rarely apart," Parker explained, lifting Olivia into her arms.

"They're joined at the *heart*," Wade added, running his hand over Olivia's fur. "Can we take her home?" he asked.

"I think so," Officer Franklin said. She grinned. "Obviously we don't have any way to contain her. The bars in the jail cells are too far apart—she could skinny through those. And her being a lock-picker, not to mention a demolition expert—yeah, I think the department would be safer without her here." She became more serious. "Listen, we have your contact information. We'll let you know what transpires from here. Hopefully that demented woman will pull her life together and leave you and poor Olivia alone, but I wouldn't be surprised if she tries to lay a lawsuit on you."

Parker shook her head. "Now that would not be fun, but it's something I can deal with, as long as Olivia and I are together and I know she's safe."

The officer ruffled the fur on Olivia's head as Parker held her. "It's been a trip, pretty girl." She tilted her head and asked, "Do you have any interesting articles coming out?"

Parker's eyes widened. "Well, we'll be spending some time in San Francisco on a case. A friend and her cat, Rags, might help with that one."

"Rags?" the officer squealed. "The klepto cat from up north of Frisco?"

"You know Rags and Savannah?" Parker asked.

"I know Detective Craig Sledge, and I've read some of the newspaper articles about his work with that cat. Gosh, Olivia, you and Rags make me want to get a cat."

Wade shook his head. "I don't think you want one like those two. They're pretty smart and clever, but along with that comes a lot of trouble and strife, right Parker?"

Parker grinned. She hugged Olivia, kissed her on the top of her head, and said, "I love this fur-being to pieces, but I'm afraid my brother's right. Be careful what you wish for, Ms. Franklin."

"That was one unusual Christmas Eve," Elaine said as she sat on her deck sipping coffee with her two children the following morning. "I look forward to a more normal holiday next year." When Wade and Parker exchanged looks, Elaine asked, "Well, don't you two? Wouldn't you like to go back to having a more normal and sane Christmas?"

Wade sat back in his chair and grinned over his coffee mug. "What would that be like, Mom? I don't remember us ever having a sane and normal Christmas celebration."

"Yeah," Parker said, "what do you consider normal?"

"Traditional," Elaine said.

"We aren't traditional people, Mom, with traditional lifestyles," Parker said.

Wade chuckled. "Yeah, what other family do you know with a famous cat whose middle name is trouble and who can even manage to get herself arrested on Christmas Eve? You don't see that scenario on commercials or even sitcoms depicting a traditional family Christmas."

Parker chuckled, "Right. Most families sing carols around a beautifully decorated Christmas tree and enjoy a lovely uninterrupted dinner."

"What do you mean?" Elaine asked curtly. "We've had a lot of traditional family Christmases. Don't you remember when your grandparents used to join us and…"

Wade choked on his coffee, coughed, then said, "Yeah, I remember the Christmas when one of Parker's barn cats came running through the house chasing a rodent or something…"

Parker burst out laughing. "It was a snake— one of those red racer snakes. Grandpa opened the door to go out and dump the turkey grease, and Smokey tripped him up. It took forever to catch the cat and the snake and get that grease cleaned up." She chuckled. "By then the food was cold." She pointed at her mother. "You were not happy that year." Before Elaine could react, Parker continued,

90

"And what about that time crazy Wilma Nelson from down the street came knocking on the door saying my cats were holding her dog hostage and wouldn't let him eat his turkey treat."

"Yeah," Wade said, "we were rounding up cats for an hour."

Elaine grimaced. "Those cats of yours, Parker—they were always causing problems."

"They weren't *my* cats," she countered. "They were the barn cats. I just managed them and played with them when I felt like it." She sat forward, toward Wade. "That's the year you taught me how to talk to them."

"That's why it took you so long to bring them home from poor Wilma's house," Elaine said. "You two sat out there like zombies trying to get those practically wild cats to listen to your brain talk."

"Mind talk," Wade corrected. He grinned, then added, "Hey, what about the time Aunt Sharlene and Uncle whatever-his-name-was..."

"Yeah, she always brought a different uncle to Christmas," Parker said.

"Which is why I quit inviting her," Elaine said disgustedly. She grinned. "Are you thinking about the time Aunt Sharlie and..." she giggled, "... Uncle whatever-his-name-was got into that awful fight out on the front lawn?" She covered her face with her hands. "Lordy, was that embarrassing."

"And the time we all looked forward to Grandma Minnie bringing her famous fruit salad," Parker started. "You know, the one with those tiny marshmallows."

"And she arrived without the salad," Wade said. "She left it cooling in her fridge at home an hour's drive away."

"I guess you're right," Elaine said with a sigh. "We do seem to have calamity Christmases around here."

"Maybe we should do Christmas at a different time of year—say, in June," Parker suggested.

"So you think it's the time of year that's the problem?" Wade asked, disbelieving. "I think it's the combination of personalities."

"Or the place," Parker suggested. "Maybe if we move the venue."

Elaine grinned and pointed. "I think it's the two of you."

"What?" Parker yelped, glancing at her brother.

"You two create an atmosphere for trouble," Elaine said. "That's what I think."

The siblings sat silently for a moment, then Wade said, "So would you rather we'd celebrate apart?"

Parker jumped in. "Yeah, Mom, are you saying that you want us to come at different times?

You think things would be calmer, quieter, more normal?" She grinned impishly, "How boring!"

Wade invited a high five, and Parker reciprocated.

Elaine rolled her eyes and took a sip of her coffee.

"Where's Pamela?" Parker asked. "Sleeping in?"

"She left early," Elaine said. "She has friends close to the city that she wanted to see."

"So, is she moving in here with you?" Wade asked.

Elaine nodded. "For now, I guess."

"Are you sure that's a good idea, Mom?" When Elaine looked at him, Wade said, "Well, it's not like you actually know anything about her— who she has become over these many years."

"I agree," Parker said. "Even *she* said she's had a rough life. That might mean she's learned to steal and take advantage of people. In fact, she's probably very good at taking advantage of people."

"Pamela is family, kids," Elaine explained. "Yes, she's had it rough. Maybe I can help her get a foothold in life." More brightly she added, "She's really interested in my new party-planning venture. She may want to join us. Lara hires extras for the larger projects."

"Does she work?" Parker asked.

"Who?" Elaine asked.

"Our new cousin," Parker said curtly.

Elaine nodded. "Off and on. She's had a variety of odd jobs—nanny, census-taker, warehouse worker, driver, telemarketer..."

Parker frowned. "Ugh." She grimaced. "I wouldn't tell people that if I were her."

"What?" Elaine asked.

"That I ever worked as a telemarketer. I think most of us are beyond fed up with those people. I mean, wouldn't you like the opportunity to take your telemarketer-frustrations out on someone—an actual telemarketer? If someone told me they make a living as a telemarketer, I'd probably slug him." When the others looked at her blankly, Parker said, "Think about it, your dinner, your meetings, your relaxation, your work are constantly being interrupted by those annoying unsolicited phone calls, and you have no recourse. They're robots, so where's the satisfaction in telling them off or slamming down the phone?" She leaned forward excitedly, inadvertently disturbing Olivia. "Hey, there's a product idea—anyone looking for a product idea? Want to become an inventor and make a lot of money?"

"What are you talking about?" Wade asked, lifting Olivia onto his lap. "You want to be a telemarketer?"

"No!" Parker insisted. "I think someone should create a telemarketer replica—you know, like that old bounce-back toy we kids used to play with. You could beat that thing up all you want and get at least some of your frustrations out. I'm even getting text-marketer messages now."

"What?" Elaine asked.

"Solicitors are including me in group texts, so when the other people in the group respond, saying, 'Stop!', 'Who are you?', or whatever, I get all those texts, too." It is sooo annoying! I'd sure never let anyone know I'd ever done telemarketing work."

"Have you?" Wade asked, impishly.

"No!" Parker insisted. She sat back in her chair, took a sip of coffee, and asked her mother, "So is Pamela homeless?"

"Didn't you hear her talking about that last night?" Elaine asked.

Parker shook her head.

Wade said, "She was in her room scheming on how to get her cat back." He petted Olivia. "And by golly she did it, didn't she, Patches?"

"Both of you seem to accomplish just about anything you put your heart to," Elaine said.

"Put our heart to?" Parker repeated. "Yes, that about sums it up, doesn't it?" She smiled at Olivia as the cat chewed a button on Wade's denim shirt, then asked, "So, Mom, what is Pamela's situation?"

"She'd been living in New Mexico with a family she met at a concert," Elaine said. "They were looking for a nanny, and she told them that was her profession."

"Is it?" Parker asked.

Elaine shook her head. "I don't think so. I think she was just looking for a place to live away from the chaos where she'd been living—which was in a halfway house."

"For drug addicts?" Parker asked.

Elaine said, "I got that it was sort of to help people graduate from homelessness to a more normal life." She looked at Wade and asked, "Isn't that how you understood it? It sounded like a good opportunity, and Pamela took it."

Wade chuckled. "It seems she lives off opportunities."

After a brief silence, Parker said quietly, "Isn't that true for most of us? It's important to keep your senses alert to opportunities."

Wade thought for a moment and said, "Then there are opportunists—people who take advantage. There's a line there, don't you think so?"

Instead of responding to Wade's question, Elaine said, "Well, whatever kind of situation it was, it got her off the streets, and now she has a job and a place to stay."

"What kind of a job?" Parker asked.

"She's a stocker at…" Elaine started.

"A stalker?" Wade asked. "She stalks people? Can you get paid for doing that?"

"No," Elaine said emphatically. She chuckled. "She's a shelf stocker at a company near Los Angeles."

"And she'll be staying here?" Parker confirmed.

Elaine nodded. "For now."

"Mom," Parker scolded.

"She's my sister's kid," Elaine said. "Lori and your grandmother would want us to take care of her. I have plenty of room, and she's good company."

Wade smiled at his mother. "Well, I hope it works out for you both, Mom. But if you need any help—I mean if you feel you're getting in over your head or that you're being taken advantage of, you call me. I'll come out here and set things straight."

Elaine grinned at him and tried not to sound too patronizing when she said, "Okay, Son. I'll remember that. Thank you."

"Mom," Wade said, changing the subject, "why would someone move to Malibu and not live on the beach? I can barely see the ocean from here. Isn't that the reason people live at the beach, to be close to the ocean—to wake up hearing it and seeing the magic it brings?"

Elaine smiled. "My, aren't you philosophical this morning." When he didn't respond, she said, "Actually, I don't like the sand all that much. Sure, I get sand here, but it's not being blown and tracked into the house all the time. I like the climate here

97

and the people who live here—they're not all stuffy like some of Gregory's friends and associates." She shuddered and lamented, "Oh, those dreary and sometimes dramatic dinners and fundraisers that bunch of attorneys are involved in. I never felt comfortable in that environment. Here, people are more relaxed and down to earth. I can hear the ocean and smell it and walk down to it anytime I want. It's win-win. A perfect place for me." She asked Parker, "You enjoyed growing up here, didn't you?"

"Yes, much more before you sold off the lot where my cats lived and where I could swing and ride my bike and practice my dance routines. Remember that cement slab Papa-Greg built for me to practice my routines? The only thing missing was room for a horse."

"You had a horse," Elaine reminded her. "She was within bicycle-riding distance, and you got to ride every day that you wanted to—you and your friends."

Parker nodded. "Yes, I did. It was a good life, Mom."

"But life doesn't always go the way we hope or plan or expect, does it?" Wade asked.

Parker faced him. "Why would you say that? Is something wrong?"

"No," he insisted. "I'm just reminiscing a little. Yeah, a part of me still wishes Mom and Dad had stayed together so we could have grown up together, but things turned out okay. I'm happy." He looked at Parker. "Don't you ever think about what might have happened if...?"

Parker shouted, "Veronica! Are you still pining over Veronica?"

"No," he said, but not very convincingly. When Parker grinned at him he backpedaled and admitted, "She *was* my first love."

"After your horses and cats..." Parker interjected. "And what about that crazy mule you used to have?"

Ignoring her, he continued, "I really believe, sometimes, that I should have married her and settled down."

"And given me some grandbabies?" Elaine said brightly.

"Maybe," he said.

Parker laughed. "No, Way-Way. You don't mean that."

"Yeah, I sorta do," he said.

"But Wade, you're a free spirit," Parker said. "Marriage would have ended that. You, tied down to a nine-to-five job and a batch of kids in an apartment someplace," Parker said. "Naw. I can't see it. You made the right decision."

He scoffed. "What makes you think it would have been one of those traditional, stifling marriages? There's no one map for relationships. A relationship is whatever the couple makes it. I know people who live way outside the traditional and still make it work."

Parker stared at him for a moment. She shook her head. "But you and Veronica? No. Not in this lifetime." She took a breath and leaned toward her mother. "I am concerned about Pamela, though."

"In what way?" Elaine asked.

"I just wonder what she expects from us. What does she have in mind? Can we actually fill the void she seems to have—you know, make things up to her? We sure can't give her back what she lost. Just like your life with Dad or Wade's life with Veronica, it's gone, and she can never get it back— none of us can. I hope she realizes that there's no retrieving what's lost, and that the only option is to start anew from where she is today." Parker sat back and tilted her head. "If we could go back I'd probably…"

"What?" Wade blurted, sitting up straighter and facing her. He caught Olivia as she started to slide off his lap. She jumped down to the deck and stared at him, then climbed up into an empty chair under an umbrella and proceeded to take a bath. Wade glanced at the cat, then asked his sister, "Are you about to dredge up your past with that polo star?" He shook his head. "No, Par-Par, don't go there. That was never meant to be."

"I happen to think it was an important turning point in my life," Parker said.

"How so?" Elaine asked, surprised. "As I remember it, you were miserable in that relationship—moody, teary, cranky. There seemed to be nothing right with it."

Haughtily, Parker said, "Well, maybe so, but I think that experience made me a stronger person. It helped put me on the path I'm on today, and, believe me, I'm living life to the fullest and loving the thrills and the challenges and the rewards."

Elaine patted her daughter's knee. "Well, I'm sure glad."

Wade grinned at his sister and shook his head, then asked, "So Mom, do you have a strategy for working with or helping Pamela?"

"I haven't had much time to think about a strategy. So no, I guess I'll just play it by ear with her—take her lead and do it one day at a time."

"Sounds kind of loosey-goosey to me," Parker grumbled.

"So what do you think I should do," Elaine asked, "give her a list of chores and a curfew, check her bag for contraband each time she comes and goes?"

Parker laughed. "Might not be a bad idea. You heard her say she was arrested for damaging government property. Who knows what else she's done or might do?"

"Well, I know one thing I might be able to do to help her," Elaine said. "She has a dream."

Taken aback, Wade asked, "Like Dr. King?"

Parker slapped at her brother and asked, "What is it, Mom?"

"She'd like to manage a museum or maybe be a museum curator," Elaine said.

"Really?" Parker asked, surprised. "What an odd thing to aspire to."

"Yeah," Wade said, "I've never known anyone with that goal. How did that happen? I mean, has she done that type of work before?"

"She told me she has spent time in museums, because she likes being around all that old stuff. She says she likes the musty smells and the way things are organized to tell a story or to make them more interesting to look at." Elaine leaned forward a little. "She liked it so much that she found a way to volunteer so she could spend more time in that environment."

"So what's her game plan?" Parker asked.

Elaine chuckled. "You always get to the point, don't you, Par-Par? How will she make this work? What's the first step?" she mimicked.

"Of course," Parker said. "Isn't that how you get from point A to point B—you know, meet your goals?"

"She has actually done some schooling toward her BA," Elaine said.

Surprised, Parker raised her eyebrows. "Really? Boy, she has had a diverse life. I wonder how she managed that—I mean, being able to go to college."

"I think someone at the museum helped her," Elaine said. "I told her I'd help her complete it. Hopefully she'll be able to take it from there."

"Mom," Wade started.

Before he could continue, however, Donny appeared at the gate. "Good morning," he called. "Got coffee?"

"Sure do," Elaine said. "Come in, Donny." She sat up and looked in his direction. "Is Cecilia with you?"

"No, she's making a grocery run," he said.

"On Christmas Day?" she asked.

"We have company coming this afternoon, and with all that happened yesterday, we didn't get a chance..." he started.

Elaine stood up and walked toward the patio door. "You drink it black, don't you?"

Donny nodded. He glanced down at his feet. "Alejandro followed me over. Do you think your cat will mind?"

"No," Parker said. "Olivia will probably be happy to see a being that resembles her."

"Huh?" he questioned.

"Another cat," Parker explained.

"How's the little boy?" Elaine asked, handing Donny a mug of coffee. She stumbled a little and squealed, "Oh, hello, Alejandro. I didn't see you there. Come to visit my grandcat? You be a gentleman now. Remember she's a lady."

Before anyone could react, Olivia stood up, arched her back, and hissed at the Maine coon cat.

"You'd better be careful, Olivia," Wade said, "he's an awful lot bigger than you are, you pipsqueak."

"It's all fur," Donny said.

When Wade reached for Olivia, Parker said, "Leave her alone. She's just setting the ground rules." She ran her hand over Olivia's fur. "A lady's gotta take care of herself, huh, pretty girl?"

Everyone watched as Alejandro crouched in front of Olivia's chair. She lay back down and blinked her eyes a couple of times.

"I think that was an invitation, buddy," Wade said. "Go for it, Alejandro."

Everyone chuckled when the tabby jumped up into the chair next to Olivia and began licking her cheek.

"They are so darn cute," Parker said, taking a couple of pictures.

"Yeah," Wade said, "Parker, you need to get her a companion. It appears she'd like to have a cat friend."

She rolled her eyes. "Yeah, sometimes. Other times she has no use for other animals or people, for that matter." She asked Donny, "How's the little boy, do you know?"

He nodded. "Cecilia visited him at the hospital. The kid's actually been put into the system just like his older sister, at least until they can do a full investigation. Meanwhile, it looks like we might get temporary custody of him. We're licensed to do foster care, you know."

"That's good to hear," Elaine said.

"Yeah," he said, "and it's a good thing the cat found him when she did, because he was under the influence of some drug and needed serious treatment." He shook his head. "Cecilia feels awful. She'd been giving the boy the juice his mother brings for him, and come to find out Arianna was putting something in there to make him sleepy. She instructed Cecilia to give it to him almost every day after his nap, but of course we didn't know it was anything but juice." He smiled. "If everything goes as we hope, we'll foster both Oliver and his sister until his mother straightens up or gives them up."

"Congratulations," Elaine said. "It appears this is something you and Cecilia both want."

Donny nodded.

"Parker, why do you keep looking at your phone?" Elaine asked. "You must have pulled it out twenty-five times since we've been sitting here."

"Huh?" she muttered. "Oh, I'm expecting a call from the police station. I still don't know if there will be more trouble for Olivia."

"That reminds me," Donny said, "the doctor told Cecilia that there are no cat bites or scratches on the boy at all. I heard that Arianna was trying to cause trouble with some wild accusations, but Dr. James, a colleague of mine, has made it clear in his report that Arianna's claims are unfounded."

"Thank heavens," Parker said, relaxing in her chair. She picked up her phone again.

"Now what are you looking for?" Wade asked, chuckling.

"An apology for Olivia from that Sergeant Sheffield."

Chapter Four

Parker ran her hand over Olivia's fur as she drove north from Malibu the following day. She was quite sure the cat wasn't interested in anything she had to say, but she felt like expressing her thoughts, anyway. She chuckled, thinking, *That's one nice thing about cats; they're pretty good listeners.* She glanced at Olivia. *I love it when she sits up in her car seat and watches out the windows.* "The world goes by awfully fast, doesn't it, pretty girl? Sorry about that. We'll stop in a while at Aunt Sharlie's, and everything will slow down. I promise."

She smiled when Olivia looked at her and mewed. After a few moments she said, "Well, that was another interesting Christmas. Actually, that was only your third Christmas, wasn't it, Olivia?" She chuckled. "We celebrated your first Christmas in January because some of us had whacky schedules that December. You and I had been together for only a few weeks then, and you hid practically the whole time we were at Gramma's." She frowned. "So it wasn't a very pleasant Christmas for you. The second one you charmed the socks off everyone. But there was that issue with you running away and that awful neighbor claiming you ate one of her chickens." Parker shuddered and kept the rest of her thoughts to herself, finally saying, "We've had some nice visits with your Gramma throughout the year, though. Remember, that's when you met Alejandro. You two were crazy lovebirds, you know it?"

Parker smiled. "Yeah, it was good to see everyone. You are a charmer, my love. I'm so glad you're such a good girl and that you're so much more relaxed when we visit family and friends. Well, you're just a social kitty-cat." She ruffled the fur on Olivia's head as she drove and muttered, "Most of the time, anyway." She took a sip of her coffee and said, "I'm sorry that policeman took you away Christmas Eve, but I'm pretty sure it was harder on me than it was on you. Yeah, you little scamp, you turned that awful mess into a fun adventure, didn't you? You even found a warm place to curl up and take a nap. Truth be told, you probably weren't too excited to see me show up."

She shook her head and continued, "What you didn't know, my pet, was that you were most likely on your way to kitty-cat jail—the place where they lock up naughty, wayward, and unwanted cats and dogs. No, I don't think you'd like that. Be glad that Mommy rescued you."

She smiled at the calico, then turned up the radio, saying, "San Francisco, here we come. Are you ready to boogie with some new cat friends and a bunch of new human friends who love cats? Oh, Olivia, you're going to be the center of attention, I just know it. You and Rags." She glanced at her phone screen. "Speaking of Rags, that's Savannah calling." She activating the Jeep's hands-free feature. "Hi, Savannah. Did you have a nice Christmas?"

"It was wonderful," Savannah said. "It was a bit hectic, but then every day around here is a little hectic. How about you?"

"Same," Parker said. "Nice, but a little wild at times."

"Did Wade join you?" Savannah asked.

"Yes," Parker said. "That was the highlight. He sends you and your family his…" she chuckled, "…greetings, I guess you'd say. He wants to be remembered to you."

"That's nice. Thank you. So where are you?"

"Just leaving San Luis Obispo," Parker said. "I have to stop at my aunt's house near Monterey."

"Didn't you stop there on your way south from here last week?" Savannah asked.

"Yes," Parker said, "I thought that would be enough, but she called and wants Olivia and me to help her with a project that only the two of us can do. I haven't a clue what it is, but I told her I have just so much time that I can spend there. I have a meeting set up for tomorrow in San Francisco."

"With the ladies of the streets?" Savannah asked.

"Of the *street cats*," Parker corrected, laughing.

"I wonder how they got that name. The cats are actually in a wooded area, aren't they?" Savannah asked.

"Yes, as I understand it," Parker said. "Well, the predecessors to this group of gals started feeding stray cats decades ago. Originally, the cats were scavenging in neighborhood garbage cans, having kittens in abandoned cars, and begging at the back door of restaurants. A group of ladies attempted to keep an eye on the cats, even back when they were running loose on city streets. So Ladies of the Street Cats was a fitting name. Can you imagine the dangers for those cats in the city? At some point concerned citizens managed to lure them into a safer environment away from traffic. Once the cats were accustomed to being fed there, they stayed, but I guess it took some convincing, from what Flo told me. She and Alma are two of the longest-standing volunteers in the group."

"Did they start the organization?" Savannah asked.

"No," Parker said. She laughed. "You'd make a good interviewer. That's one of the first questions I asked. It was actually a woman who ran a café in the city. She lived rurally and already had a bunch of cats on her property, so she'd take

110

home the more friendly strays that were hanging around the alley behind the restaurants. Evidently the street cats created big problems for restaurant owners. They had to make all sorts of concessions to discourage the cats—devise cat-proof covers for their trash bins, for example. Even then they had cats hanging around at all hours of the day and night. That café owner—I believe her name was Cora—led the crusade to encourage other restaurateurs to leave appropriate food out for the cats, but only during specific hours."

"Makes sense," Savannah said. "So the cats were conditioned to come only at certain times— they were fed—and they stopped dragging trash out and making a mess."

"Yes," Parker said, "and over time, Cora and a small group of cat advocates moved the majority of the cats on to Cora's property, and the Ladies of the Street Cats became Ladies of the Forest Colony."

"That was when, in the fifties?" Savannah asked.

"Yes," Parker said. "One thing led to another, and a somewhat cohesive, dedicated group was formed to care for the cats. Actually, I believe the colony now congregates on or near the original property where the restaurant owner lived. As I understand it, there was a wildfire, then flooding in that area, and Cora lost her home. No one ever built there again. Most or many of the cats survived those catastrophes and lived to reproduce again. So there are many generations of cats. It's only in recent years—say the last twenty, maybe—that these gals have been running a spay-and-neuter program."

"How many are there" Savannah asked.

"Cats or ladies?" Parker asked.

"Both," Savannah said.

"As I understand it there are around twenty-four cats in the core group and five dedicated colony managers," Parker explained. "They have a membership of around fifteen."

"Did you ask the ladies about the stuff the cats are digging up?" Savannah asked.

"Yes, but apparently they don't want to get me involved in that right off the bat. In fact, Flo was so evasive I'm surprised the editor who hired me knew about it. They do have a detective working with them, and even he has agreed to keep the lid on that situation for now. I'll drill him once I meet him—that is, if we click and trust each other."

"So you haven't talked to him, yet?" Savannah asked.

"No. When do you think you and Rags will be free to join us on this mission?" Parker asked, adding, "Since I won't be diving into the meat of our adventure right away, we might hold off on you coming until early next week. Why don't you give me the weekend? I'll let you know when it feels right for us to start involving our cats. Sound good?"

"Yes; however, you know there will probably be some library and newspaper research necessary to find out something about the people who the stuff belonged to. Do you think we'll have access to police records," Savannah asked, "so we can get in touch with the families of those people who went missing? By the way, have they dug up anything that identifies any of those people? Or are we simply dealing with an abandoned homeless encampment?"

Parker chuckled. "Hey, you've done this type of thing before, haven't you?" She took a deep breath. "Like I said, the gals I've talked to are primarily concerned with the cats at this point. They'll probably have to move the cats, and I doubt I can conduct decent interviews with those ladies until the cats are safe. So…"

"So what?" Savannah asked, suspiciously.

"So I told them that you and I can help with that—you know making sure the cats are safe before word gets out about what's showing up on the colony site. That's pretty much where we are at the moment," Parker said.

"Okay. I'm willing to help with the cats. It sounds like there will eventually be an excavation going on out there, and we sure don't want to subject the cats to that chaos." Savannah paused, then asked, "So did you get a place?"

"Yes. It looks perfect, according to the videos they sent me. There's no real view or anything, but the location is good for our purposes, and it looks comfy—two bedrooms, nice kitchen." Parker said.

"Great. Of course, I'll pay half for Rags's and my stay."

"I was counting on that," Parker said. "So listen, traffic's getting heavier, and I want to keep my mind on the road. Let me get us settled, hopefully tonight. I'll give you a call once I get the lay of the land, probably sometime tomorrow. Sound good?"

"Purr-fect," Savannah quipped. "Travel safely, and good luck."

"Thanks. See you soon."

It was a little after three Friday afternoon when Parker pulled onto her Aunt Sharlene's property. She turned off the car engine and looked at Olivia. She smiled when the calico opened her eyes and blinked a couple of times. "You had a good nap, didn't you? Are you up for a kitty-cat visit?"

Olivia stood up and stretched, her fluffy tail arching over her back. She looked through the windows and let out a couple of chirpy mews.

Parker laughed. "Are you ready for a break, sweetie?" She unfastened Olivia's car-seat restraint and attached the leash to her harness, then picked up her purse, opened the car door, and urged Olivia to follow her. Instead, the cat put her paws against the

114

dashboard and peered out through the windshield. She meowed loudly, then looked at Parker. "What is it, Olivia?" Parker asked. She tugged at the leash. "Come on. Let's go visit Aunt Sharlie. She probably has a treat for you."

Olivia meowed excitedly and leaped from the car, pulling hard against the leash.

"Oh, so you're eager to get a treat, are you?" Parker said. She trotted after the cat, chuckling. "Well, Aunt Sharlie will be pleased to know how excited you are to see her today, or is it all of her kitty-cats you want to see?" Rather than follow up the walkway toward the front door with Parker, Olivia veered in another direction, pulling against the leash. "Where do you think you're going, Miss Sassy Pants?" Parker asked, picking up the cat and carrying her up the porch steps. She knocked on the door twice. After a few moments, she muttered, "Hmmm, she's not answering. Her car's here; maybe she's out back." She lowered a wriggling Olivia to the ground "Is that what you're trying to tell me, that she's out back? Okay, show me, Olivia." When Parker tripped a little along the cobblestone path, she yelped, "Olivia, slow down."

The cat continued to pull. She led Parker along the side of the house and around to the back, where Parker stopped and looked across the yard. "I don't see her." When it appeared that Olivia was leading her out to the clothesline, Parker said, "So you think she's hanging clothes out here? No, she

I doesn't use that old clothesline anymore. Maybe just to hang freshly washed quilts and blankets on a sunny day." She stopped. "Olivia, I don't want to go out there in the dirt. I don't want you getting all dirty, either," she said, picking up the cat. She glanced around. "You know, she could be next door visiting the neighbors, or she took a walk. Want to go see the kitties? The kitties are over there in their outside pen."

When they approached the pen several of the cats pawed at the wire mesh toward Olivia, but she showed absolutely no interest. Instead, she leaned in the opposite direction and struggled to get down. Parker finally lowered her to the ground and shook her head. "I don't know what your problem is, girl, but you're making me mad." When Olivia continued pulling, Parker said, "Okay, little missy, show me—and it had better not be a lizard or a snake." She let out a deep breath and scolded, "Olivia, I'm not kidding. I don't want to see any reptiles." Suddenly Parker stopped. She looked at Olivia. "Did you hear that?" she asked, moving closer to an old shed on the property. "What was that? It sounded like…" She walked along with Olivia, holding tightly to the leash. She was surprised when the cat bypassed the door and ran around to the back of the shed, where she stopped. Parker gasped. "Aunt Sharlie! What happened?"

"Oh my God," the woman said, "I thought you'd never get here. Listen, you'd better call 911.

I came out here without my phone, and I'm pretty sure I broke my darn leg."

Parker looked around. "Doing what?"

"Well, you're not going to believe it," Sharlene said, "but I caught me a burglar."

"What?" Parker asked, frowning. "Where?"

"In the house. After I hit him over the head with my shoe, I came out here to get some rope or wire or something to restrain him, then I planned to call the cops. They can sometimes take a while to respond, you know, and I didn't want him to slither away."

"Slither?" Parker repeated. "Are you talking about a snake?"

"No!" Sharlene said emphatically. "A burglar. A man or a kid. He's kind of skinny. I caught him in the act!" she bragged.

"No kidding? When did this happen?"

"About an hour ago, I guess," Sharlene said. "I don't have my watch on."

Parker looked toward the house. "And you think he's still knocked out?"

Sharlene grinned impishly. "Probably not, but he's not going anywhere. I'm pretty sure I fixed it so he won't be able to get out of the predicament on his own."

"What did you do to him?" Parker asked. "Where is he?"

"Under the couch," Sharlene said, matter-of-factly.

"What?" Parker shrieked.

"Yeah, while he was knocked out I moved that big old couch over him. There's no way he can skinny out from under that thing."

"Aunt Sharlie, that couch has only a few inches clearance." Parker glanced toward the house. "You could kill someone putting a heavy couch like that on him."

"Nah," her aunt insisted. "Like I said, he's pretty skinny. He'll be okay. Even if he isn't, he deserves the pain. Did you call 911?"

Parker took her phone from her purse and asked, "What's your address here?"

"Give that to me," Sharlene said, "I want to order an ambulance, too. I don't think you can get me to the hospital, not with my leg all broken like this."

Once Sharlene had ended the call and handed Parker her phone, Parker pointed. "Who put that splint on your leg?"

"I did," the woman said. She reached for Parker's hand. "Help me up, will you?"

Parker stepped back. "Oh, I don't know about that, Aunt Sharlie. If that leg's broken, I don't know how I can get you up by myself without hurting you. I think you should stay put until the paramedics get here."

"Get out of here!" Sharlene spat. "Do you think I want anyone to see me like this? Get me up."

Parker let out a sigh and said, "How about if I go next door and ask Dave or one of his sons to help?"

"Yeah, I guess. Okay, go."

Parker picked up Olivia and started to walk away, then stopped and announced, "The police are here. I'll tell them to go in the house, okay?"

"Get me up first," Sharlene called.

Parker considered her request, and said, "I think they'd better check on that poor man under the couch." She hesitated and shook her head. "Aunt Sharlie, I can't believe that you…" She let out a deep breath and continued walking swiftly toward the house to let the police officers inside. She then trotted next door, returning minutes later with a young man. "Aunt Sharlie, I let the police in, and..."

"Hi, River," Sharlene said. "Are you going to help Parker get me up?"

"How do you expect to walk on one foot?" Parker asked.

Sharlene thought for a moment, then said, "There are some old crutches in the shed there. Bring those to me."

It didn't take the pair long to get Sharlene up on one foot and walking with the crutches. She said, "Thanks, River. You can go back to your hogs now. Tell your folks hello for me."

"Now where do you think you're going?" Parker asked her aunt, walking along beside her with Olivia on her leash.

"To see if the police found that guy," she said.

"Well, I think we need to stay out here." She glanced around and saw a step stool leaning against a shade tree. She opened it and said, "How about you sit down on this stool. It should be easy enough for you to get up off of it." She motioned to the paramedics, who had just entered the property. "Over here."

"What happened?" one of them asked.

"I broke my leg, that's all," Sharlene said. "If you'd just splint it proper like, then I need to find out if the police have that burglar-thief in custody. I'll be ready for a ride to the hospital after that." She turned to Parker. "You'll stay and feed the cats won't you? They'll expect their supper around five."

Before Parker could respond, the older of the paramedics said, "Well, let's take a look at you, ma'am. You're Mrs. Ingram, right?"

Sharlene nodded.

"I'm Jonathon," the paramedic said. "My partner here is Lucas. So you injured your leg?"

"Yeah, it's broken. I'm pretty sure of that."

Jonathon gazed at Parker. "Did you make this splint?"

"I did it," Sharlene asserted.

"*You* did?" Jonathon moved aside a little. "Look at this, Lucas. She's used rebar and twine and what's this fabric?" he asked.

120

"Burlap from an old sandbag," Sharlene explained.

Lucas shook his head. He asked, "How'd you hurt yourself, Mrs...?"

"Sharlie. Just call me Sharlie. I came out here to get some rope to tie up that sneaky intruder, and I guess I tripped over some of that stuff I keep meaning to pick up. There's just too much clutter around here. Gotta take care of that." She glanced at Parker. "My niece found me."

"It was Olivia," Parker said.

"Olivia?" Lucas repeated. He looked around. "Is that another niece?"

Sharlene laughed and nodded toward the calico. "It's this beautiful cat." She asked, "Olivia found me?"

"Yes," Parker said. "She started freaking out as soon as we drove up, and she dragged me out here to the shed. I fought her all the way, thinking she was just being obstinate."

"Gotta listen to the animals," Lucas said.

Parker watched as Jonathon cut away her aunt's makeshift splint, then asked Lucas, "You're an animal person?"

He petted Olivia. "Yes. I'm actually working on my prerequisites for veterinary school."

"From paramedic to veterinarian, huh?" Sharlene asked.

The younger man nodded. He watched as Jonathon examined Sharlene's leg. "I came across

121

an accident a few months ago—it was awful. A truck pulling a horse trailer was hit by a semi and I actually got involved in helping with the horses because they and a couple of dogs were in worse shape than the people were. I've always been an animal lover, and this just put me over the edge. It gave me the nudge I needed to make the commitment to my original dream."

"Good for you," Parker said.

Jonathon grinned at Lucas. "Tell them what got you sidetracked, Lucas—you know, from that original dream."

"Well, I got into a bit of trouble and had a debt to pay because of it. When it was all over, I had time to think and I decided I wanted to help people. I knew Jonathon, and he talked me into becoming a paramedic. I had no idea I could do something that big—learn to be a paramedic. Where I come from that seemed to be an impossible leap—from street thug to part of a valued profession."

"A thug?" Sharlene questioned. "You have such a nice appearance. I can't imagine you being one of the bad kids on the block."

"Oh, I was a two-bit trouble-maker, I guess you'd say." When two policemen approached with another man in tow, he turned to look.

The others also watched with interest. Everyone remained quiet except for Sharlene. She called out, "Good; you got that no-good thief."

"Mrs. Ingram," one officer said, moving closer, "how are you feeling? I hear you got hurt in the confrontation."

She glanced toward the second policeman, who stood a distance away with the suspect in cuffs. "Oh no, that creep didn't hurt me. I tripped and fell in the yard out there trying to get a rope down from a hook." She shook her head. "I should have waited for my niece to get here. She stopped by to help me with some things this afternoon."

"A rope?" the officer questioned suspiciously. "And what were you going to do with the rope, may I ask?"

"Tie him up of course," Sharlene said. When she saw the look on his face, she laughed, "Oh, you thought I was going to hang him from the nearest tree? That's funny."

He grimaced. "Well, anyone who would throw a sofa on someone like that, I don't know what else they might do." He moved closer. "I have a few questions, if you don't mind. Do you feel like talking?"

"Sure, it's just a broken leg. I'm fine," Sharlene insisted

"Actually, ma'am," Jonathon said. "I don't think it's broken. I'm going to splint it and suggest that you go to the emergency room for an x-ray, but I think you just have a sprain."

"Oh!" she exclaimed. "Well, that would be good news." She asked, Parker, "Can you take me to the hospital?"

"Sure," Parker said.

"So what do you want to know, Officer?" Sharlene asked.

He let out a breath and glanced toward the house. "How did you manage to put that man in the predicament we found him in? He said you did that."

"How does he know?" she asked, grinning. "He was knocked out. I knocked him out with my shoe."

"Do you mean you kicked him?" the officer asked.

Looking sheepish she said, "No, not exactly. I found him, you see, all scrunched down looking in my refrigerator. Can you imagine? I haven't cleaned it out all week. I don't need a snoop getting in there and rummaging around."

Parker grinned and rolled her eyes.

"How did you…" the officer started.

"Well, I hit him and he fell over," Sharlene said, "so I dragged him into the living room and moved the couch on top of him." She grinned. "Pretty clever, don't you think so?"

"That thing's heavy," the officer said. "Are you saying you did that all by yourself?"

"I live alone," she said. "How do you think I clean under there or get a shy kitten to come out? Yeah, I can move it. You have to know how to manage that sort of thing so you don't hurt yourself."

"Did the gentleman take anything?" the officer asked. "Or did he threaten you in any way?"

"He may have taken a pear. I thought I saw him pocket a pear. And I want to press charges. Strangers can't go around walking into people's houses like that stealing fruit."

"Did he take anything else?" the officer asked.

"I don't know. I'd just come in from feeding the cats, and there he was going through my refrigerator. Did you find anything else in his pockets?" Sharlene asked.

"Just that pear," the officer said. He glanced at his partner, then asked, "Mrs. Ingram, have you ever seen the...um...burglar before?"

"I don't think so," she said, shrugging. "I didn't recognize him from the back. Although I didn't spend a lot of time looking at him because I was so shocked to find someone in my house like that."

"Well, we'd like for you to take a look at him, if you don't mind," the officer said.

"Look at him?" Sharlene said in disgust. "I don't know. Can't you just take him to your jail and not bother me with that? Like I said, I only saw him from the back. He went down face first, and I put the sofa on him. Never did see his face."

"Well, ma'am," he said hesitantly, "he's claiming that he knows you and that he was invited here."

Sharlene sat rigid. She frowned and glanced in the direction of the accused. "He said that? I don't think I did. Yeah, but maybe I'd better take a look. I hope I don't know the man—I can tell you I sure didn't invite him into my house. I came in from out back and there he was already inside," she repeated.

The women watched as the second officer walked toward them with the suspect. Sharlene grabbed Parker's arm and held on tightly. As they got closer she squinted, gasped, and said, "Arnold!" She buried her face in her hands. "Oh no. I'd forgotten that you were coming by." She spoke more softly, "...to get pears. Oh no, Arnold..."

Ignoring her, the suspect said, "Hi, Parker."

"Arnold, how are you...I mean..." Parker stammered. "Are you living here now? I mean in the area?"

He shook his head.

"Good god," Sharlene said, "how could I have forgotten that you were coming over today? I need to get myself some of that medicine that helps your brain remember things better." She ordered, "Officer, remove those handcuffs immediately. That's my nephew. He and his father—my deceased first husband's brother—are in town for a car rally, and I know how much Arnold likes those fancy pears you order through the mail. I met them for dinner last night and told Arnold to come by and get some." She shook her head. "How in the world I forgot that, I don't know." She reached her arms out to Arnold.

He hesitated, then simply squeezed her hand.

"I'm so sorry. Are you hurt, Arnold?" she asked. "Did the paramedics look at you? Oh god," she whined, "I'm going to be the black sheep of the family, if I'm not already. Officers, please go back to your work. I'm sure you have more important things to do than cater to a foolish old woman. Thank you for coming so soon. Good bye, now."

"So you're not pressing charges?" one officer asked.

"Why would I do that?" she asked, dismissing the officers with a wave. "Parker, would you go get that box of pears from the fridge? I put the best ones in that box for Arnold."

"Sure." She started to leave with Olivia, who pulled against the leash. "You want to stay with Aunt Sharlie?" she asked.

Arnold reached out. "I'll hold on to her for you." When Olivia strutted up to him, he kneeled and began ruffling her fur. "Aren't you a pretty girl?" He looked up. "We had a calico like this in the neighborhood once. She spent so much time at our house that her family gave her to us. I really liked that cat, but boy, was she a stubborn little twerp."

Savannah grinned at Arnold. "Yes, they can be obstinate." She spoke more quietly, "Like our aunt."

Either ignoring her or having not heard her, Sharlene asked, "Arnold, do you know how to manage cats? I mean, Parker and I are going to trim my cats' claws this afternoon. We could sure use some help."

"Sure," Arnold said. "How many cats do you have, Aunt Sharlie?"

Parker grinned. "You don't want to know."

Sharlene slapped at her. "Oh Parker, there are only nine, and five of them are as tame as newborn kittens."

"Arnold," Parker said, "you look like a deer in headlights." She patted his shoulder. "It's okay, Aunt Sharlie has protective gear." She faced their aunt. "Let's get you inside and comfortable, and Arnold and I'll bring the cats in one by one. Is that a good plan?"

Sharlene cheered. "Yes!" She stood up, with help, and said to the paramedics, "Thank you for coming. I'm glad to know it's only a sprain."

"Well, that's my educated guess," Jonathon said, closing up his equipment bag. "I strongly recommend that you have that x-rayed."

"Yeah, yeah," Sharlene said, making her way toward the house with Parker and Arnold on

128

each side of her. "Arnold, you can probably take me to the hospital later, can't you? Parker's on her way to Frisco this afternoon."

The young man nodded.

Without missing a beat, Sharlene said, "You know, since I have you two here, we might as well treat the cats to a spa day—you don't mind combing out mats and maybe bathing a few of the dirtiest ones, do you?"

Parker and Arnold rolled their eyes at one another. He said, "Of course not, Aunt Sharlie, as long as you don't forget who I am during the process and throw that couch down on me again."

"Okay," Sharlene said, sitting down at Parker's insistence. "Fill the kitchen sink with a few inches of warm water, will you? Nail clippers are on that shelf above the sink. Get a couple of towels off the stack there on the table. Is everything ready?" she asked. When Parker and Arnold nodded she joked, "Then go get our first victim." The others had just walked out the back door when Sharlene shouted, "No-No! Olivia, no! Parker!" she screeched.

"What?" Parker asked, returning to the kitchen. "Have you changed your mind about which cat you want first?"

"No," Sharlene said, pointing. "We already have our first customer right there."

That's when Parker saw Olivia lounging in the sink of water. "Oh, Olivia," she complained, reaching for her.

"Wait," Sharlene called, picking up her phone. "I want a picture of that. Who would believe a cat would volunteer to get a bath. Oh my gosh, she's rolling over. Olivia, do you realize you're getting wet, or can't you feel the water through all of that fur?"

"She knows," Parker said. "She likes water, especially if it's just the right temperature." She plucked the cat from the sink and placed her on a thick layer of towels, then grabbed another towel and began rubbing her fur. "Olivia, darn it, you just had a bath a couple of days ago and a couple of days before that." She wrapped the towel around her and cradled her in her arms.

"Want me to blow dry her?" Sharlene asked.

"I think I'll just let her air dry," Parker said, lowering her to the floor. "I need to get on the road before too long, so let's not get sidetracked." She put her hands on her hips and scowled down at the calico, who began frantically licking her fur. "Olivia, sometimes you wear on my patience. Now you stay out of the way, will you?"

"There it is," Parker said, turning into a driveway later that evening. "This is our home for the next month, Olivia." After parking the car, she lowered

Olivia to the ground, picked up her purse, and walked toward the front door, stopping once to look around. "Seems to be a decent neighborhood," she muttered. "Shall we go inside?" She leaned over. "Flo said she'd leave the key here under the blue pot."

She'd just picked it up when she heard, "Excuse me! Excuse me! Are you Ms. Campbell?"

"Yes," Parker said, turning to face a spry woman who appeared to be in her seventies.

"Welcome," the woman said, approaching quickly. "I can't tell you how thrilled we are to have you here." She shook Parker's hand. "I'm Flo. We spoke on the phone." She looked down at Parker's feet. "This must be Olivia. Oh my goodness, she is a beauty." She laid a hand on Parker's arm. "I mean, we have some beautiful cats in our colony, but the long-hairs certainly don't keep themselves as beautifully coiffed as Olivia, here." She squatted and petted the calico. "She's soft, too. You've lived every moment of your life in luxury, haven't you, my dear?"

"You might be surprised," Parker said, quietly. "As a matter of fact, she comes from sad and meager beginnings."

"Oh, I'm sorry," Flo said. "Well, it appears you have it made now, you beautiful doll." Flo looked up a Parker. "She's so lovely. She must be a real girlie-girl."

Parker chuckled. "Wrong again. Yeah, she's a tomboy. I've had to give her three baths this week already."

Flo stood up. "My, my. I guess looks can be deceiving." She smiled. "Well, she's a beauty." She took a quick breath. "I don't want to hold you up. I'm sure you'd like to get settled. You drove all the way up from Santa Monica?"

"Close," Parker said. "Malibu."

"Well, you get settled. I'm afraid I took liberties and put some groceries inside for you. I made you a chicken and broccoli casserole and a nice salad, and I stocked your fridge with a few things—eggs, milk, bread, butter and coffee and tea. Oh, and a few bottles of fresh drinking water."

"How nice of you," Parker said. "Thank you so much. Let me know what I owe you."

Flo shook her head. "Like I said, we're just awfully grateful that you could come. I have a feeling that your being here will make all the difference to our colony cats."

"And you believe this because?" Parker asked.

Stunned for a moment, Flo explained, "I understand that you'll be interviewing us for an article. We can certainly use the publicity. You see, we run on donations. We may have to move the cats which would be quite a large project. We'll need funds and a suitable place for them." More quietly, she said, "Alma and I believe that your coming

132

here at this time is more than a coincidence. You were sent to fulfill our needs—the cats' needs." She shimmied. "We're so excited we can't even begin to tell you."

"Oh," Parker said, "that reminds me, I brought some information to show you what a forward-thinking woman up north has done to protect a colony of feral cats. It's a wonderful solution for the cats she's caring for."

Flo looked suspiciously at her. "Well, if it involves borders and boundaries, I doubt it will fly here. Our cats have been free for decades. Of course, the original cats are gone after so many years—you know, over the rainbow bridge—but many of these are ancestors of free-roaming cats. They've been feral for generations. So if there's fencing involved, your solution probably won't be the answer we need."

Parker smiled. "We'll see." She bowed slightly and looked down at Olivia, who seemed to be getting restless. "Thank you again for greeting us and for leaving food. Gosh, I sure didn't expect that. Olivia and I'd better get unpacked and settled. We're meeting first thing in the morning, right?" She pulled out her phone and scrolled through her texts. "Eight thirty at five-five-three Bartlett Street?"

"Yes. It's just around the corner. You and Olivia might want to walk. In fact, come out about eight twenty and I'll walk you over there. Alma, has the largest home, and we generally meet there."

"Did you say Olivia's invited?" Parker asked.

Flo smiled. "Oh yes. When we did our due diligence, so to speak, and we learned about some of the things your Olivia has done and how close the two of you are, we're as excited to get to know her as we are you. Yes, bring her, if you don't mind."

"Okay," Parker said. "Thank you again. See you tomorrow."

The following morning Parker and Olivia found Flo waiting for them on their front pathway. Flo chuckled. "She seems so comfortable wearing that harness and being attached to a leash. Does she go everywhere with you?"

"Pretty much," Parker said. She grinned down at the cat, who was sniffing everything in sight from the end of her leash. She admitted, "Olivia can be a little destructive when she's left alone." She winced. "I hope she didn't disturb the neighbor next door with her morning ritual."

Amused, Flo asked, "What's her morning ritual?"

"Well, once she's good and awake, she starts flying through the house screeching like a banshee." Parker leaned toward Flo as they walked together down the sidewalk. "Not that I actually know what a banshee sounds like, but I imagine it's a freaky, shrill sound like Olivia makes when she's in her freaky, ADHD mood." Parker continued, "Yeah, she just tears around the house, leaping at the walls, jumping over anything that gets in her way. On our hardwood floors, she slips and slides all over the place." She chuckled. "She needs a set of four kitty-size sneakers in order to get traction on those slick floors, although I think she gets a thrill from doing her slip-and-slide routine."

Flo chuckled. "Sounds like she suffers from fits of the zoomies with a little added flair." She grinned. "A banshee, huh? What do you do when she does that?"

"Stay out of her way." Parker giggled. "It's a riot. Sometimes I follow after her picking up things she has sent flying." She glanced at Flo as they walked. "By the way, I love the décor in my condo, but I've already undecorated in there—you know, I put the vases and bric-a-brac in drawers and cabinets, where they'll be safe for our stay. I hope the manager doesn't mind."

Flo smiled. "Well, I'm the manager, and I sure don't mind." She looked down at Olivia as she walked along on her leash. "She doesn't look like the little bulldozer you describe."

"She's not, for the most part," Parker said. "She just has her moments. She's actually pretty good to take someplace, but I do have to keep an eye on her."

"Here we are," Flo said, motioning toward a large home with a well-kept front yard.

"Oh, this is nice." Parker said quietly, "I hope the homeowner doesn't mind my bringing a cat with me."

Flo laughed. "No problem. Absolutely no problem. Come on. You'll see what I mean."

Flo was right. The splendid house was definitely cat-proof and cat-friendly. Alma Schmidt greeted the women at the door and graciously invited them inside. "Oh goodie," she said, "you brought the beautiful Olivia. Flo showed us a video of the two of you just last week, and we all fell in love with Olivia. Can I pet her?"

"Certainly," Parker said. "She loves attention."

"If she's like my cats," Alma said, "she craves attention until she doesn't. Then she becomes elusive, reclusive, and rude." She leaned closer, adding, "Especially the calico and the tortie."

Parker laughed. "You've nailed her." She glanced around the room. "Oh, my gosh, this is wonderful. Olivia, do you see what I see? A kitty-cat jungle gym." Parker turned in place, trying to take it all in. "Amazing. Magical." She started to ask, "Can she…?"

"Absolutely," Alma said. "Take that apparatus off her and let her go. My cats are congenial. Juliet can be a little snooty, but from what I've seen and heard of Olivia, she can hold her own."

Parker nodded. "Yes. She had to fend for herself for a while before she was plucked off the streets. She may seem demure, but she can stand up for herself."

Alma watched as Parker removed the harness, then the hostess picked up Olivia and said, "No squabbles now, okay, Miss Olivia? I already had a talk with my guys and dolls." She pointed to perches and kitty-cat-size staircases running all along two of the walls in the large, sunny room. "You can do all the climbing you want. There's Juliet. Watch out for her. It may take you girls a few minutes to come to terms with who's top cat." She pointed. "That's Garth Brooks and Xavier. Seymour is sitting up on top. See him? Over here are Harriet, Lucille, and Daphne. Everyone," she said, "this is Olivia." She faced Parker. "I had an Olivia once, but she didn't stay long. She just didn't fit in with my guys and dolls."

"Guys and dolls?" Parker repeated. "I'm surprised they aren't Frank Sinatra, Marlon Brando, Vivian Blaine..."

"Oh my, you're too young to know about *Guys and Dolls*. You must be a movie buff."

"Somewhat," Parker said. "I have a good memory for details like that."

Alma raised her eyebrows for Flo's benefit. "Interesting. Well, here come the rest of the group.

Flo, want to let them in while I show Olivia de Havilland to the lower staircase." She asked Parker, "Or is she Olivia Newton-John or one of the villainess Olivias?"

"It depends on which day you ask me," Parker quipped.

"Whew!" Parker said, dropping into a chair in her condo a few hours later and unfastening Olivia's harness. "What a morning." She ran her hand over Olivia's fur. "You must be tired after the climbing you did with all your new cat friends." When Olivia plopped onto her side in front of Parker, she laughed. "Yeah, exhausting, right? Well, you have a nap; I need to call Savannah and tell her the plan." When Olivia rolled over onto her back, Parker tickled her tummy. "Yes, we have a plan. And you're going to have company. Want to see Rags again? He's coming to visit you." She pulled her hand back quickly when Olivia grabbed it and began kicking it with her back feet. The cat then rolled over onto her feet and trotted off toward the kitchen.

"Are you hungry?" Parker asked. "I'm sure not. Not after all those goodies the ladies of the street brought." She followed the cat into the kitchen and checked her kibbles and water-bowl levels. She giggled, while adding kibbles and refreshing Olivia's water. "Ladies of the street," she muttered. "That cracks me up. In reality, they're just a wonderful bunch of women—gutsy women, I might add, who love cats and want to help those that can't help themselves. I'd say they're doing a pretty good job of it, too." She ran her hand down the cat's back. "Hey, that reminds me—get your rest, Olivia; we're going with Flo and Alma later today to see the colony and meet some of the feral cats."

As if she understood, Olivia mewed.

"Hi, Savannah," Parker said into the phone moments later. "Are you busy? Let me re-phrase that; I know you're busy. Do you have a few minutes to talk? Is this a good time?"

"Sure," Savannah said, chuckling. "I've been reorganizing toys, books, and games all morning—you know trying to fit in all those the kids got for Christmas. I'm ready for a break. The kids are having a snack. Michael's with them to make sure they have some fruit along with their cookie treat."

"I wish I had someone to slap my hand when I dive into the chip bag or the cookie jar," Parker said, laughing.

"Oh, I can't imagine that would work with you," Savannah said, "not as independent as you are. I could see you rebelling—'I'll eat as many chocolate chips as I want.'"

Both women laughed and Parker said, "Savannah, I'm afraid you've nailed me."

"So did you meet with the ladies of the street?" Savannah asked.

"Yes," Parker said. "Well, five of them. Oh Savannah, what an interesting and boisterous group of women."

"Boisterous?" Savannah repeated.

"And mostly pretty savvy," Parker said. "There are a few…" she started.

"There are in most groups." Savannah snickered. "We can't all be fabulously brilliant and clever."

"Right," Parker said, laughing.

"So what's the plan?" Savannah asked.

"Olivia and I are meeting some of the gals at the colony site this afternoon. Oh, they gave me a copy of their journal."

"Their journal?" Savannah asked.

"They have a historian. She's the sweetest gal. She's in a wheelchair, so she doesn't often go out to the colony. She's a retired professor who loves research and cats, and she has collected a lot of the colony's history through newspaper articles, interviews with past participants, and so forth. She actually found an original log kept by former members as far back as the sixties. They kept track of the cats' comings and goings, traumatic occurrences—you know, like attacks by coyotes and other predators, and even human harassment, hassles with neighbors and the county—all sorts of things. So they have a pretty detailed accounting of

140

the happenings in that colony for most of the time it's been in existence, as well as the people who cared for the cats."

"Wow!" Savannah said. "That's amazing. I don't think anyone has ever documented things related to any of the colonies I've been involved with. What a boon for your article. You know, Rob…"

"I was thinking the same thing, Savannah. Rob may very well want to film a documentary up here. Let's take care of business first, before we get him involved, shall we?" Parker suggested.

"You're the boss," Savannah said. "Sure." More quietly she said, "If we're able to resolve the mystery of the missing persons and the things showing up out there where the cats live, Rob will definitely be interested in *that* story."

"Oh yes," Parker said.

"So what did you find out about that so far—anything?" Savannah asked.

"Not much," Parker said. "It's not even written into any of the documentation—you know, the journal. When I brought it up I got the idea that the ladies really don't want that kind of publicity. They have that detective involved, but for the most part, they want to keep a lid on what they've found in order to protect the cats. That sort of publicity could destroy all they've worked toward. They certainly don't want a barrage of people traipsing through the cats' home or heavy equipment disturbing their serenity—not until they're able to move the cats to a safer location, and that could take time."

"Where are you exactly?" Savannah asked.

"Outside the city," Parker said. "It's easy to see that the cats could be in jeopardy, as they're experiencing suburban sprawl out this way. The women are pretty stressed. They're having a hard time seeing the light at the end of the tunnel." More guardedly, she said, "Savannah, they're counting on me to make it happen. They think the publicity from my article might just be their saving grace— you know, getting word out about the history of the colony and the good work they're doing with the cats and all."

"Did you tell them about June's cat ranch?" Savannah asked.

"Yes. I showed them the pictures I took and did my best to describe it to them. They loved the concept—well, some of them did. Others are turned off by the fencing. I think they need to see and experience it for themselves. I also got the impression they can't see themselves ever being able to acquire such a place. We have work to do in order to get them from point A to point B."

"What seems to be the problem?" Savannah asked.

"Well, I think there are so many women who have been in the group for so long that they're kind of stuck in their thinking. They've run low on fresh ideas and they're resistant to trying something new. The gals, for the most part, are older. They're tired, but they don't want to let go of the cats or their ideals or the way things have always been. Know what I mean?"

"I think I do," Savannah said. "They want to protect the cats without having to step outside their comfort zone." She continued, "What they may not understand is that in order to have achieved the success they seem to be experiencing with the cats, there had to be changes made along the way—you know, compromises, new thought, new ideas..."

"Certainly," Parker said, "and I think we need to find out which of the gals are the most forward thinking and most highly thought of in the group. That's who we need to work with."

"An influencer, huh?" Savannah said. "Well, it sounds like you have your hands full there."

"We!" Parker emphasized. "*We* have our hands full, but what an opportunity."

"Yes, for you and for the cats," Savannah said. "You'll be gathering information for your article, and I guess, among other things, we can maybe help them come up with some fundraising ideas. Once they see the video I put together of the cat ranch..."

"Oh!" Parker yelped. "You got it done? How'd it turn out?"

"Great!" Savannah said. "But it sounds like we'll also need some sort of sales pitch or incentive to help the women understand how important fundraising is. This is one area where they might have to go above and beyond their comfort zone, that is if they hope to raise the money they'll need. It'll mean reaching out into the community and finding ways to attract donations from the corporate world."

"Yes!" Parker cheered. "Even a membership drive might help the situation. I'd like to see them bring in new blood to move the more inflexible, short-sighted folks off dead center."

"I'm loving it," Savannah said. "So do you think we can make it happen? I have some fundraising ideas that have been successful here, but to get the corporate world involved and maybe a land donor would take another level of technique. That's why I think a documentary might be important. It would reach deeper into the community, country, and world and maybe touch a nerve somewhere. All they need is the right kind of participation and money, of course."

"But what comes first, the chicken or the egg?" Parker asked, thinking out loud. "We don't want word to get out about the mystery because it will disturb and maybe harm the cats. We can't move the cats to protect them until they have a place to go. And we can't advertise the need for funding or find a potential land donor until the mystery's cleared up."

"Why?" Savannah asked.

"What?" Parker questioned.

"Why do we have to wait until the mystery is resolved to do fund-raising?"

Parker explained, "My sense is that with publicity, people will want to visit the colony—you know, out of curiosity and to see how well it's being operated. This would undoubtedly blow things wide open out there. Word would get out about the things they're finding, then here would come the authorities and the media. This would attract looky-loos. No, it could be detrimental to the cats if they start a publicity campaign before the mystery is resolved. Heck, Savannah, there could be bodies buried out there, for all we know."

"Oh!" she yelped. "Yeah, I see your point. We sure don't want to put those cats or the women in jeopardy, but then if this is the site of a mass murder or something, the families of those people need to know. They need closure." She let out a deep sigh. "It will be a mighty tricky tightrope walk, won't it?"

"Yeah," Parker said, "it means we'll have to work smart and work fast. When can you be here?"

"Is tomorrow soon enough?" Savannah asked.

Chapter Five

"Hey," Parker greeted when she opened the door to Savannah and Rags midday on Sunday. "How was the drive?"

"Not too bad," Savannah said. "Any day traveling without the chatter, fussing, and complaining of small children is a good day of travel." She winced. "Although I started really missing them after about an hour of peace and quiet."

Parker laughed and ushered Savannah inside. "Hi, Rags," she said, leaning over and petting him. "Did you have a good trip?"

"Yeah, he slept mostly. He wouldn't even share the driving duties, that one," Savannah joked.

Parker chuckled. "Olivia prefers to be chauffeured, too." She glanced around the room and called, "Olivia, you have a guest." When the calico didn't emerge, Parker invited, "Come on, I think I know where she is."

"How dazzling you look there on that princess pillow, my sweet girl," Savannah crooned, seeing the calico stretched out across an eyelet pillow. She ruffled the fur around Olivia's neck, and smiled when Olivia rolled over onto her back and began to purr.

Rags seemed happy to see Olivia too, and he jumped up onto the bed with her.

This caught the calico off guard, though, and she quickly stood up and arched her back.

"Olivia," Parker said, "it's your friend, Rags. Don't you recognize Rags?"

"Well, he came on a little strong," Savannah said, "interrupting her nap like that. Rags," she scolded, "tone it down there, boy."

Parker chuckled. "She's fine, aren't you, Olivia?"

At that, Olivia stretched with her paws out in front of her, arching her tail across her back.

"Wow!" Savannah said. "That's quite an impressive pose, Olivia."

"Yeah," Parker said. "That's one of her signature yoga moves. Don't you love it? Hey, let's bring in your things and get you settled. The detective will be here in about twenty minutes."

"You've met the detective?" Savannah squealed. "What did you find out?"

"He was out at the colony site yesterday when I went out there with some of the gals. He seemed eager to talk to us," Parker said, She asked, "Did you eat lunch?"

"I did," Savannah said. "I grabbed a turkey sandwich at a deli a little while ago."

Once Savannah had freshened up and she'd hung her blouses and slacks, she joined Parker in the living room, asking, "So have you seen some of the things that are showing up at the cat colony?"

Parker shook her head. "Not yet. I guess they've been picking up that stuff—you know, treating it as hazardous material—and they're hiding it at an undisclosed location."

"What?" Savannah said. "That's odd, isn't it? You mean they're disturbing what could be the scene of a crime or a burial ground?"

"So your theory is that those things were left there and not that they were brought there and dumped?" Parker asked.

"Oh, well, I don't know. I got the impression that they've maybe been there for a while, and that the cats or some other animal or just erosion is suddenly uncovering them," Savannah explained. "Isn't that what you believe?"

"I'm not sure," Parker said. When she heard a knock on the door, she stood up, opened it, and invited in a man who appeared to be in his late fifties. "Detective Judson Caldwell?" she asked.

"Yes."

"Come in, please." She stepped aside. "I'm Parker Campbell, and this is Savannah Ivey."

"Hello," he said, shaking her hand and Savannah's. "You can call me Jud." He looked down at Savannah's feet and smiled. "Rags, I presume."

Savannah picked up the grey-and-white cat. "Yes. You know him?"

"I know Detective Craig Sledge," he said. "Every time I see him, he shows me pictures of that cat."

"No kidding?" Savannah said, amused.

The detective nodded. "Yes, Ms. Campbell told me you were coming with the cat. I'm most eager to see him in action." He chuckled. "He doesn't seem to be very active now. Is it his nap time?"

"Even a famous gumpaw needs his rest," Savannah quipped.

"*Gumpaw*," Parker repeated. "Good one." She invited, "Please sit down, Detective. Can I get you something to drink?"

"No. I'm fine. Okay if I sit here next to the pretty cat?" he asked, nodding toward where Olivia lay on the arm of an overstuffed chair.

"I'm sure she'd love it," Parker said. "She's partial to men."

"Good to know," he said.

"Are you a cat person, Mr. Caldwell?" Savannah asked. When he looked sternly at her, she said, "I mean, Jud...Detective..."

He grinned, then shook his head and admitted, "Never gave cats much never mind until I hooked up with the cat ladies and met some of their cats."

"The feral cats?" Savannah asked.

"Those and some of their own cats," he clarified. "I've been actually thinking about dragging home a cat in need—something I can buddy up with on cold and lonely nights."

Savannah smiled. "I think you'll be glad you did." She sat on the edge of the sofa. "So tell us what's going on out there at the colony—I mean with the stuff that's been showing up."

"Well, as I told Ms. Campbell, I happen to be a friend of the Thorntons." He glanced at the two women. "Nancy is one of the cat ladies. She found the first few items and called me. That was three weeks ago and I've been working sort of behind the scenes hoping to figure out what's going on without creating issues for the women and their cats. Those ladies are pretty serious about the cats. They don't want to upset them, so we're working under the radar, so to speak. Once the cats are moved, and I guess you ladies are going to help with that, then we can go full steam ahead and try to resolve that growing mystery."

"It's growing?" Savannah asked. "In what way?"

"Well, more stuff keeps showing up, apparently involving more people—you know, we find another name or identity among the stuff," he explained. "I've possibly identified belongings from five people so far."

"And all five of them have been reported missing?" Savannah asked.

The detective gazed at her for a moment, then confirmed, "Yes. Yes, and all right around, if not exactly at, the same time."

"Now what do you mean?" Parker asked. "You told me that yesterday, and I've wondered about it. Do you think we're dealing with a mass murderer?"

The detective thought for a moment. "Possibly, but I think it's more bizarre than that—more peculiar, perhaps, and most definitely unexpected. I think this case may go down in history as one of those unsolved mysteries." When Parker and Savannah looked at him quizzically, he said, "It's just too weird and convoluted. You see, there are items being dredged up—some very personal items—belonging to people who have never met, according to the research I've done, yet who may have all disappeared under the same circumstances at or about the same time. Doesn't that seem peculiar to you? I mean, are we talking about alien beings beaming them up?" When the women looked at each other wide-eyed, he said, "Yes, so far this thing is that level of spooky."

"Wow!" Savannah muttered after a long silence.

Parker raised her eyebrows and said nothing.

"What research, may I ask?" Savannah blurted. "I thought you were keeping this discovery under wraps."

The detective cleared his throat and adjusted his position. "Yes, to protect the cats, but I've been going through police files and newspapers, hoping that something will click between that research and what we're finding—you know, that I'll discover a common denominator. You ladies should know that so far my research is *my* business. I'm taking a personal leave and trying to get a head start on reopening the investigation." He chuckled. "The original investigation led us nowhere. Absolutely nowhere—certainly not to a cat colony. We could find nothing to connect the missing people except for the fact that several of them apparently disappeared at exactly the same time."

Savannah sat silent for a moment, then asked, "And you want us involved because?"

"Oh, that's easy," the detective said. "Because of your cats and your work within this realm—well, maybe not exactly this realm, but you know what I mean—mysteries—mysterious occurrences. I hope like heck there's a reasonable explanation for what's going on and for what happened all those years ago, but so far..."

When his voice trailed off, Savannah asked, "How long ago did those people go missing?"

"Most of them were reported missing within days of each other. Family members gave accounts of their last phone conversation with their loved ones being within minutes or hours of others whose family member went missing at seemingly the exact same time. Some people weren't reported missing until days or weeks later. Some of those might have been caught up in whatever happened that night."

"Why would you come to that conclusion?" Parker asked.

"Well, some of those people weren't as connected to their families. Some were homeless, you see. Family members were accustomed to their homeless sons or daughters staying away for days, weeks, months. According to one transcript, their teenager had a history of running away or just disappearing for days. Was that kid involved in the same disaster or mass murder as the other ten, or…?" He looked into Parker's eyes, then Savannah's. "And after all this time there has been zero evidence or clues as to what happened to those eleven-plus people until possibly now."

"Whoa," Parker said.

Savannah shook her head.

"See what I mean, ladies?" he asked.

"Yeah," Parker said, "eerie."

"Yes," Savannah muttered, "a mystery for sure."

"So who wants in and who wants out?" the detective asked. "Anyone ready to go home?"

"Not on your life," Parker said with enthusiasm.

"I'm in," Savannah confirmed. "So what's the first step?"

"I'd like to take a look at the stuff that's been showing up," Parker said.

The detective nodded. "Agreed and done. I have it in my shop."

"You do?" Savannah asked. "You didn't leave it where it was found?"

He nodded. "Yeah, I have it. I also have newspaper articles, transcripts from some of the interviews with family and friends, as well as names and numbers."

"Really?" Savannah asked. "How…"

"I know people," he said. "Let's leave it at that. And it's a cold case." He laughed, "Oh, you asked when the space ship most likely came down and scooped up these folks. Next month, around the sixteenth, seven years ago."

Again the room went silent.

Finally the detective asked, "Is there anything keeping you here? Would you like to trudge over to my place and see some of the evidence?"

Savannah and Parker stood up and Parker said, "Let's go." She asked Savannah, "Want to take…"

"The cats?" Savannah asked. "I think it would be a good idea."

"I was hoping you would," Judson Caldwell said.

"Why?" Savannah asked.

"I'm curious to see them work, for one thing. If they're as clever as I've heard they are, they may be able to point out something I've missed." He laughed. "As I said, I'm working alone on this with no one to bounce suspicions and ideas off of, so I'm eager to have your input, but also the cats'. Heck, they might become part of my memoirs, if I ever stop dabbling in mysteries and crimes long enough to actually write them."

"Mr. Caldwell," Savannah said,

"Jud," he corrected.

"Okay, Jud, do you think this is a crime? Is it possible that the cat colony was the site of a horrific murderous crime?"

"I can't imagine it," he said. "Of course, I brought that up to the ladies, but it seems they've been taking care of the cats in that same place for over fifty years, and they were actively tending to them seven years ago. There's no way they wouldn't have seen something—graves at the very least. I even went back to check the weather during that time in this area. It had been unusually wet that week—in fact, that month. So no, it doesn't appear that whatever happened, happened there, and what would have brought those eleven—or more people to that spot on that particular night, anyway?" He faced the women. "See what I mean about the viability of thinking a spacecraft swooped down and beamed up those people?"

"So it's assumed that those eleven people were in the same place at the same time when whatever happened happened, right?" Parker asked. "Or could they have been—you know, killed someplace else and brought to this spot?"

"Or they gathered here and left without their belongings," Savannah said. She shivered. "Gads, this is becoming more and more creepy."

"Still with us?" Parker asked.

"Absolutely," Savannah said, putting on her jacket and fastening Rags's harness around him.

"What is this place?" Parker asked, walking toward a weathered barn with the detective, Savannah, and the two cats.

Judson Caldwell grinned. "This is my happy place." He nodded toward a modest house a distance away. "That's where I live—alone now. We bought the place years ago. My wife wanted a smaller house that was easier to keep up, and I wanted a large shop for my projects."

"Projects?" Savannah repeated. "Are you a putterer?"

He grinned. "That's not how my wife described it, but yeah, something like that. I fix things and build things. I support local swap meets." He pointed. "Did you see my bumper sticker? I brake for yard sales. I refurbish and sell antiques and other vintage items. It keeps me out of trouble and gives me a distraction from investigative work."

"Cool," Parker said.

He opened a large swinging door and invited the women inside the spacious building.

"Gosh, this *is* an old barn, or was it a garage?" Savannah asked.

"I've been told it was a shop on the original farm here, built a hundred years ago, in the twenties. I suspect it could be older—maybe an original carriage house."

"So you found an antique right here," Parker quipped.

Jud nodded. "Pretty much." He glanced around the place. "You can see it's been reinforced over time." He pounded on a wall. "It's pretty solid for being such a relic. But it's my relic, and I love it. When I'm out here working, I feel as though I've gone back in time." He chuckled. "My wife used to tell me I was born too late. She said my heart and mentality belong in another century—whatever that means. I took it as a compliment, but sometimes I don't think she meant it that way."

"It's dark in here," Parker said, squinting.

"We can remedy that," the detective said. "That's one important upgrade I made in this place—the lighting." He flipped a couple of switches. "Better?"

"Oh my, yes," Savannah said, expanding her gaze. "Way cool." She moved closer to one of the makeshift tables that lined the walls. "So is this…" she started

"Yes, I've turned part of this space into my examination room-slash-storage area." Jud motioned with his arms. "These are the things we've taken from the mystery site so far."

"We?" Savannah questioned.

"Me, the cats, and sometimes one of the cat ladies will find something and point it out to me."

"Good gravy," Parker muttered, as she and Savannah walked solemnly around the area with the cats, ogling the items laid out on the tables. "You washed all these clothes?" she asked.

"Not really," Judson said. "I wanted to leave them as close to how I found them as possible, not that it would probably matter, because they were all a-jumble, anyway, and after seven years…"

Savannah glanced at him. She focused again on the items and chuckled.

"What's funny?" Parker asked.

"I was just thinking, if those people were beamed up, they must have gone naked."

"Unless," Jud said, "they had extra clothes with them."

"Oh," Parker said, "like they were traveling when they were…"

He nodded. "Or camping."

"Camping?" Savannah repeated. "Do you think they were camping out there with the cats?"

"Not likely, I guess," he said. "Someone would have seen or heard them, but it could have been a homeless encampment. The homeless are pretty careful about being seen, and they're good at hiding their belongings." He looked into space and said, "A few of them could have been living above where you normally see the cats—up there in that heavily wooded area, but what the others would be doing in a homeless camp, I don't know."

"So at least some of the missing people were homeless," Parker asked, "but not all of them?"

The detective leaned against a table. "According to family members who were originally interviewed—you know, those who reported their loved ones missing—yes, some of them were considered homeless. Those who checked in with family occasionally or often were easier to identify as possibly missing. Certainly some of the families that eventually claimed their homeless loved one went missing along with the others that night were grasping at straws—you know seeking closure in a way, and holding out hope at the same time." He grimaced. "Now, after going through this stuff, I believe at least some of those families could be right."

"Really?" Parker asked. "How's that? Are you saying that you can discern differences between belongings from the homeless and the ordinary citizen?"

"Good question," he said.

Parker quipped, "I'm a professional interviewer. It's what I do."

"Well," he said, walking briskly to a box of shoes across the room, "the answer is yes." He picked up a couple of the shoes. "See, these have holes worn in the bottom, and twine in place of shoelaces. That's something a homeless person might wear, right? And look at this; it's a state-issued ID card that most homeless carry…if they want government handouts, that is." He looked down at the card in his hand and said, "This gal wasn't reported missing until a few years after whatever happened that fateful night."

"So it *could* have been a homeless encampment?" Savannah asked.

"I doubt it," Jud said, "because most of the people who were reported missing at that time were not homeless, and after learning a little about some of those people, it's unimaginable that they'd be in a homeless camp—you know, feeding the homeless or just hanging out." He shook his head. "It doesn't make sense." He faced the women. "None of it makes sense, especially since this seems to involve such a mix of people. You girls are going to talk to some of the families, aren't you?"

"We hope to," Parker said, "but aren't you concerned that will blow your cover? You want to keep this stuff a secret, don't you? I know the ladies do—at least for now."

He nodded. "Yes, I do, but no, your visits with the families won't create any red flags. They're used to the attention. They're approached by reporters and magazine editors—even filmmakers several times a year. No, don't worry about blowing my cover. This mass discovery will remain under wraps until I'm ready to bring in the authorities."

"So why are you taking it upon yourself to recover all this stuff?" Parker asked. "From the looks of it this has been a large undertaking."

Just then, Savannah jumped. "What is it, Rags?" she asked, clutching tightly to his leash.

"Let him go," Parker suggested, when she saw the large grey-and-white cat dancing around at the end of his leash. "Let's see what he's interested in."

Savannah frowned. "You remind me of Craig Sledge. He's always saying, 'Just let him go. Let's see what he does.' Do you know how many times I've regretted listening to him?"

Parker laughed as she watched Savannah loosen her grip on the leash and allow Rags to sniff out whatever it was that seemed to interest him. She asked the detective. "What's under that table? He wants to go under there."

"Oh," he said, "that's where I store the smaller items and pieces of things I can't quite make out." He motioned toward two large tables in the back of the building. "See that mess over there?

Every morning as I drink my coffee I work on that puzzle."

"Puzzle?" Parker questioned, moving closer. "Oh," she said, upon seeing the tabletops more clearly. When Olivia reached up with her paws against one of the tables, Parker picked her up. "No you don't, sassy pants. Detective Caldwell doesn't need you messing with his puzzle." She leaned closer with Olivia in her arms. "What is this stuff?" She then said, "Oh, parts of driver's licenses, food stamps, receipts…oh my gosh, these things probably came from their pockets and purses."

Savannah walked up next to Parker, now holding Rags in her arms. The two of them stood speechless. Finally Parker said, "This kind of accentuates the reality that those people met with some sort of cataclysmic tragedy, doesn't it?" She said more quietly, "I wonder if there are clues in some of this stuff that will answer the big question."

"Which is?" Savannah asked.

"What in the hell happened?" Parker said, solemnly.

Savannah nodded and spoke more quietly. "Those people are sure becoming real. All of this is evidence that they once lived, and now…" She couldn't finish her sentence.

Parker took a deep breath and asked, "What did Rags find over there?"

"Oh, this," Savannah said, holding up a small photograph. She showed it to Parker, then the detective.

"Where did he get this?" Jud asked, snatching it from her.

"It was on the ground next to that box under the table with the t-shirts in it," she said. "Just a corner of it was sticking out, and it was face down. Do you know who that is?"

Jud stared at the weathered picture, then held it to his chest and choked up. "Yes. This is my daughter." He swallowed hard and slumped. Speaking more quietly, he said, "Hannah went missing about the same time as the others, but my wife and I held out hope that she simply ran off to live a different kind of life somewhere, and that she's happy and she'll come home when she's finished sowing her wild oats." He looked down at the photo. "This was her student ID card; she attended the community college." He took a ragged breath. "But this doesn't mean anything. You say the cat found it in the dirt? Yeah, she probably dropped it out here before she took her trip." He looked at the women. "She liked coming out here with me. She has the curiosity gene like I do—you know, she wants to find out what makes things work, what makes people tick. She was always asking questions and digging for answers. And boy, did she love the internet." He chuckled. "She just about wore out our desktop computer with her questions." He took a deep breath. "She was nineteen when she left us."

"She left that day," Parker asked, "when all the others were reported missing?"

He nodded. "But we found out later that she'd taken her laptop and some of her clothes. Yeah, I'm almost certain that she just ran off on a whim, hoping to find…I don't know what."

"Olivia," Parker called, when the calico began pulling against her leash. Parker caught her toe against a table leg, losing her balance, and the leash slipped from her hand. "Olivia!"

"Are you okay?" Savannah asked.

"Yeah," Parker said, "she just tripped me up. She does that." She scurried to catch up to the cat.

"She's okay," the detective said. "She can't hurt anything."

Ignoring him, Parker continued following Olivia and found her underneath another table pawing at something in a large cardboard box. "What did you find, girl?" she asked.

Suddenly the detective shouted, "No!"

Parker quickly picked up Olivia and looked at the detective quizzically.

"I don't want anything in that box disturbed," he insisted.

"Some of your puzzle pieces, huh?" Parker asked, walking away from the area with Olivia.

"Something like that," he murmured. He quickly led the women and the cats across the room toward the open door, saying, "Well, now you've seen what we're finding. I'll go to the house and get you the material I told you about so you can do some of your own research if you wish."

"Oh my gosh, was that freaky," Parker said later as she and Savannah shared a snack back at the condo.

"You mean about the detective's daughter?" Savannah asked "Do you suppose that's why he has become so involved in that case? He wants to find out if his daughter was caught up in whatever happened."

"And hoping like heck she wasn't," Parker said solemnly.

"So much so that he might actually be misplacing and ignoring clues that she was, indeed, involved," Savannah said. "I mean, he was sure protective of that one box Olivia wanted to investigate. Do you think it's related to his daughter?"

Parker shrugged. "I don't know, but the fact that Olivia was interested in it is telling, if you ask me." She winced. "Poor guy."

"I know. How awful it must be to lose someone and not ever know what happened to them." The women sat with their thoughts for a few moments, then Savannah asked, "Did you look over the contact list he gave us?"

"Yes. Now let's hope it isn't too outdated," Parker said. She glanced at her watch. "Shall we make a few calls? We have, what, a half hour before we meet the gals at the colony site."

"The ladies," Savannah corrected, laughing. "Yeah, give me part of that list and we can both make calls."

Parker chuckled. "What if we make appointments for the same time? I'll call a couple and see if we can make some appointments for later today. Okay with you?"

"Yeah. I wonder if any of them still live in the area. If not, we can maybe do video calls."

"Good idea," Parker said, picking up her phone. It wasn't long before found Savannah and the two cats taking in the sun in the small backyard. "Are you sure they can't get out?" she asked.

"Look at that wall," Savannah said. "Olivia's agile and clever, but she can't scale a wall like that, can she?"

Parker shook her head. "Not that I know of. Yeah, this looks like a great yard for cats, actually."

"Only not enough flowers and butterflies to suit Rags," Savannah said. She turned to face Parker. "What did you find out?"

"Well, I actually made contact with a few people. We have an appointment with a couple whose mostly homeless son may have gone missing around that time. They're one of the families that contacted police weeks after the others were reported missing. Apparently they typically heard from their son once a week or so."

"And they still haven't heard from him?" Savannah asked.

Parker shook her head. She then said, "I didn't notice this before, but it looks like the detective has gone through and checked the names of people whose belongings he has identified."

"How many of the people has he identified?" Savannah asked.

"It looks like just a handful," she said. "Maybe four or five."

"So is this family you talked to still living locally?"

"Yes. They're actually in the same place, waiting for their son to come home. We can see them this afternoon," Parker reported. She added, "I had trouble getting an invitation from this other gal. She's convinced that her daughter ran off with her boyfriend and got married like she and her husband did years ago, but she's willing to talk to us." She frowned. "According to the detective's notes, he has found some of this girl's belongings."

"Ohhh," Savannah moaned.

"I also got in touch with a man who now lives in Sacramento. We can do a FaceTime chat with him."

"What's his story?" Savannah asked.

"His daughter went camping with friends. I want to get the names of the friends. He sounds kind of confused. He says he doesn't know or doesn't remember if the friends also went missing." Parker pointed at a name on the list and said, "I'm curious about this family. Evidently their three boys created a small band. The notes say that all three of their sons went missing that night. They'd planned to play somewhere, but the parents don't know where. That could be a big-time clue—you know, if we could find out where the boys were playing. I definitely want to talk to those people if we can find them. I left a voicemail, but it wasn't clear whose number I'd called. Meanwhile, we might check with local clubs and see if we can find out where these kids played that night. I wonder if anyone did that."

"Their parents didn't know where they were going that night?" Savannah asked. "Do you know how old they were?"

"Sixteen, eighteen, and nineteen," Parker said. She chuckled. "They called themselves The Three Boy Band."

"Cute. So you don't think anyone checked to see where those kids were that night?" Savannah asked.

"It's surprising, the things in an investigation that are sometimes overlooked," Parker said. She snapped a few pictures of Olivia peering out from behind a flowering bush, then continued, "Yeah,

Olivia has made discoveries several times that investigators missed, and she has found things that caused them to rethink the direction of an investigation. I imagine Rags has, too."

Savannah nodded. "He sure has." She looked at her watch. "We'd better go meet the ladies of the night…" She laughed. "I mean of the street cats."

"What a beautiful setting," Savannah said, looking around the wooded area where the colony cats lived. "I don't see any cats."

Alma chuckled. "That's just the way they like it. Some of them come out at feeding time for certain of us. One tight pod—you know, cats that hang together—come out when I'm here alone. When Flo's with me, some of those hide and others will come out."

"True," Flo said, "and I see some of the cats that Alma rarely sees."

"Except as a blur," Alma said. "If we bring strangers, most of the cats will hide. They won't even come out to eat until we're gone—then we just hope everyone got what they needed."

Parker gazed toward the mountains in the background. "Do they go up into those hills? Is that part of their territory?"

Flo shook her head. "I don't think so, do you, Alma? They seem to stay down here among the trees."

"Yes, they do," Alma agreed. "As you can see, they have good cover here. I believe they feel safer down here from natural predators and people—you know, hikers and campers."

"So each of you ladies have your own groupie cats?" Savannah said. "That's interesting. I don't recall that being the case with the colony cats I've dealt with."

"Groupie cats," Alma repeated. "That's funny. I guess we do each have our own groupies."

Flo laughed. "Then there's Peggy."

Alma nodded. "Oh yes, she's a favorite among the cats." She motioned toward Olivia and Rags, who were each walking around on the end of their leashes. "Those two will probably eat her up. Cats love Peggy."

Flo laughed. "We all love her." She motioned behind Savannah and Parker. "Here she comes in her catmobile."

The two women turned. "Catmobile, indeed," Parker said, taking a few pictures as Peggy approached in an electric cart complete with small stuffed cats dangling from it and a cat-motif flag waving above Peggy's head.

"I love it!" Savannah exclaimed. She noticed, "Oh, look she has a cat with her. What is that, a Ragdoll?"

170

"She loves the Ragdolls," Alma said. "I think that's Belinda she has with her today. Hi, Peggy," she called. "Hi, Belinda."

The woman giggled. "Wrong again, Alma. This is Bailey. She wanted a ride today."

"Well, she's gorgeous," Savannah said, reaching out her hand. "Hi, I'm Savannah."

"Peggy," she said, squeezing her hand. "I've been eager to meet the two of you." She looked at Parker. "You're Parker Campbell? Any relation to the barber in town, Joshua Campbell?"

Parker shook her head. "Not that I know of." She ran her hand over the cat sitting on the seat next to Peggy. "She's a beauty." She nodded toward Olivia and said, "She's part Ragdoll."

"On the mother's or father's side?" Peggy asked.

"I don't know. I never met either of them. I learned that bit of her history from a DNA test. I swabbed her and sent it off just out of curiosity. She has traces of other breeds, too: Maine coon, Abyssinian, Savannah, Peterbald, Persian… In other words, she's a bonafide mutt."

Peggy reached down and ruffled the fur on Olivia's head. "Hi, lovely. Do you have some of those charming Ragdoll traits?"

"Well, she plops and flops," Parker said, laughing.

"Oh yes. That's certainly one of the traits."

"She's also sometimes clumsy," Parker said.

Peggy nodded. "A Ragdoll can get their growth pretty quickly, and that can cause awkwardness."

Parker asked Savannah, "Didn't you say Rags is half Ragdoll?"

Savannah nodded.

"That sleek, handsome cat?" Peggy asked, pointing at Rags.

"Yes," Savannah said. "I know the mother and she's a purebred Ragdoll. His father, believe it or not, is a good-sized orange tabby."

Everyone stared down at Rags, and he stared back.

Just then Parker pointed and whispered, "Look, here they come. The cats. I see cats."

"Because Peggy's here," Alma said.

"Look at them all," Parker said giddily. "Like some sort of cat convoy traveling across the plains."

Everyone laughed quietly.

Peggy stepped out of her cart and walked closer, leaving Bailey on the seat, her leash attached to the cart. Peggy spent several minutes looking out over the colony cats, who all stayed their distance, suspiciously watching the women. Rags and Olivia sat side by side seemingly intrigued by the feline procession.

Finally Peggy said, "They're all here. How beautiful to see them all come out together. Twenty-four. Rachel even brought her kittens. See the tangerine tabby with her two small clones? They're growing nicely, don't you think so?"

"They look great," Savannah said. "You ladies seem to be doing a good job out here."

"And I can't get over what a beautiful spot this is," Parker added.

"Too beautiful," Flo said. "It was one of the community's best-kept secrets until…"

"Until?" Savannah questioned.

"Until a group of developers discovered it," Flo said. "I was pretty sure it would happen. You can see that housing tracts have been sprawling out in this direction, getting closer and closer. It was inevitable that developers would want to encroach on this land—cut down the trees, destroy the natural foliage, and put up houses."

"Protection and regard for cats has come a long way," Peggy said, "but not far enough that any government anywhere would mandate that a cat colony be considered a sacred place where cats can live unmolested."

"Sacred, huh?" Parker repeated.

"Hell, yes," Peggy said, surprising both Parker and Savannah. She continued, "Cats were on this planet maybe millions of years before those bureaucrats that run our local and federal governments. If only cats could speak and stand up for themselves," she lamented.

"Yeah," Flo said, "we have to speak for them, and who listens to a bunch of doddering old women? They never have over all these years, and they aren't about to now."

"Unless…" Savannah muttered.

"We're listening," Flo said, moving closer.

"Well first, tell me who owns the property," Savannah suggested.

"Heirs of Cora Washington. She locked in a fifty-year lease with us, as long as this land remained a cat colony. We're enjoying a grace period now, as the fifty years was up some time ago. There's a clause in there giving us first crack at purchasing it, but land prices have gone up a whole lot more than Cora could have imagined. There's no way we can afford that inflated price."

"Unless you can bring in donations—maybe lure a large donor with a heart for cats who would purchase this property for the cats, or…" Savannah hesitated, "someone who will donate property somewhere else and build a facility like the one I believe Parker has talked to some of you about."

Alma brightened. "Yes, that place is amazing. Ms. Campbell showed us some pictures. The plans for that facility should be spread throughout cat communities worldwide."

"I think June Balcomb and her staff are actually working on that," Savannah said. "Meanwhile…"

Before she could continue, she looked down at Rags. "What is it, boy?" she asked when she felt him pulling against the leash.

"He probably wants to go out there and mingle with all of those beautiful cats," Parker said. Just then Olivia tugged on her leash and Parker said, "I guess so does Olivia. Is that what you want, girl?"

Savannah looked in the direction the cats stared and asked, "Are you sure this is all of the cats?"

"Interesting you should ask that," Parker said. "I sense it too. There's someone else in the shadows that…"

"Yeah," Savannah said. "There's something wrong, isn't there?" She pointed. "Those cats over there keep looking back behind them."

"I noticed that," Peggy said. "I wondered if there was a coyote coming down off that hillside."

"The cats would probably be scrambling if that were the case," Savannah suggested. She looked at Parker. "Shall we follow these two?"

"I think it's imperative that we do," Parker agreed. She looked at the other three women. "…if it's okay."

"If you believe there's a problem with a cat, most certainly," Flo said. "Go."

The others waited and watched as Parker and Savannah walked slowly with Rags and Olivia into the depth of the colony and disappeared. Parker was first to return. Breathlessly, she asked, "Does anyone have a carrier they can put their hands on in a hurry?"

The three women glanced at each other and Peggy said, "I live closest. Alma, is that your car? Want to go grab one off the back patio? I washed a couple this morning and left them out to dry."

"Sure," Alma said. "Be right back."

"What's the problem?" Peggy asked.

"Well, ladies, you now have four more cats, and there may be more to come." Parker said. "The dam's in pretty bad shape. Savannah's a veterinarian, you see, and she's afraid we might lose her. The cat needs veterinary help and fast." Parker glanced around at the women and asked, "Are you gals prepared to raise a litter of newborn kittens?"

"Kittens this time of year?" Flo shrieked.

"It happens," Peggy said. "Sadly, it happens."

"I know it does, but…" Flo started. She then answered Parker's question, "Yes. We have a team that takes in newborn kittens. We're pretty self-sufficient when it comes to the cats."

Peggy took a cell phone from a small pouch hanging from her catmobile. "Hey, let me call our veterinarian. She'll take emergencies even on a Sunday. That's why you want the carrier, right?"

Parker nodded.

"Oh my goodness," Alma lamented. "Four more little souls with no place to go."

176

"Yeah, that poor mother cat," Parker said. "She sure doesn't look good. She must have been a beauty in her day, before the elements got to her." She looked at Peggy. "Savannah thinks she's probably at least part Ragdoll."

"Really?" Peggy squealed. "What sort of coloring does she have?"

"She has like a dark-brown mask," Parker said. "I don't know many Ragdolls, but I thought they were mostly pointed like a Siamese or a Himalayan, but Savannah said they also come with masks. She said something about an inverted V."

"Selma," Peggy said, choking up.

"Do you know the cat? Is she part of the colony?" Parker looked up. "Oh, here comes Alma with the carrier." She took it out of the car for Alma and started to walk off with it toward where Savannah and the cats waited.

"Does she have a brown mark..." Peggy started.

"Here, I'll show you a picture," Parker said.

"Yes, that's Selma," Peggy said. "Oh my, what did those people do to her? They told me they'd had her spayed. And what is she doing out here, for goodness sake?"

"You believed them?" Alma asked.

Peggy nodded. "Yes. Otherwise I would never have let Selma go."

"Do you need help, Parker?" Flo asked.

"I think Savannah and I can handle it,"

Parker said. "That poor cat—Selma—is pretty upset."

When they returned with the cat and kittens in the carrier covered by Savannah's sweatshirt, Peggy said, "Dr. Darling is waiting for her. Here's the address. It's not far." She asked, near tears. "Can I see her?"

Parker lifted the cover and Peggy yelped. "My goodness, Selma, what have they done to you?" She covered the carrier and instructed, "Go. She's in pain." She put her hands up to her face. "Poor, poor thing. Oh, and have Dr. Darling send me the bill. I'll be the one to pick her up…if she makes it." She began to cry, "Oh, Selma, I'm so sorry."

"I'm pretty sure there are more kittens in there," Savannah told Dr. Gina Darling several minutes later. "She's pushing, and I think I can feel at least one. She's so thin, and we found her out in the brush, so we don't know how long it's been since she's eaten or had anything to drink. She's dehydrated; I tried to get her to drink water, but she seems too weak. I believe she's about to give up," Savannah explained.

Dr. Darling examined the cat and glanced at Savannah. "Are you a veterinarian?"

Savannah nodded. "On leave now, raising our children. My husband runs our clinic in Hammond."

"Dr. Michael Ivey?" the woman asked.

"Yes," Savannah said. "Do you know him?"

She nodded. "Mostly *of* him." She told her tech, "Get her ready for x-ray; I want to see what we're dealing with, and I'll want to start fluids right away."

Minutes later the veterinarian announced, "You're right, one more kitten. A big one, lying crossways. I'm going to try to manipulate it, but if it doesn't move quickly, I'll go in and take it. Want to assist?"

Savannah glanced at Parker. "Sure," she said. "By the way, this is Parker Campbell and her cat, Olivia."

Dr. Darling smiled down at Olivia, who sat at Parker's feet. "I love the calicos. I have two of my own." She tilted her head. "She looks familiar. I mean you don't see that sort of muttonchops look on many cats."

"Muttonchops?" Parker repeated.

"Yeah, her coloring—the way the black fur is sort of squared off around her jowls like that. You don't often see that wide-faced look on cats. Doesn't she do something?" She lowered her brow. "Actually, so do you. Parker Campbell." She repeated Parker's name, then said, "You're a reporter, and your cat—Olivia, right? She helps with the cases you write about. I've seen your story on some of the blogs I follow."

"Really?" Parker asked.

"Yes," the veterinarian said, "but I didn't know you rescued cats, too."

Parker grinned. "Well, it was Olivia and Savannah's cat, Rags, that found this poor girl. By the way. I guess her name is Selma. Peggy with the Ladies of the Street Cats wants to pay for her treatment and take her home when she's well."

"Yes," Dr. Darling said. "She told me. From the looks of her, that's an excellent decision. This girl's in bad shape. I sure wouldn't send her back to the people who were supposed to be taking care of her. Okay, let's get Selma juiced up in hopes that she can tolerate the surgery, if we have to go that route."

Chapter Six

"We're just going to make that appointment with Dana Boehm," Parker said, pulling her car away from the veterinary clinic.

"Yes, we got a little sidetracked with poor Selma and her babies." Savannah said into the backseat, "You two fur-babies were amazing today—saving those kitties like you did."

"Yes," Parker said. "Good job, Livvie and Ragsie." She giggled. "That's what you call him, right? Ragsie?"

"Sometimes, yes," Savannah said, grinning. "And you call Olivia Livvie?" She chuckled. "I loved hearing Teddy call her Lolivia."

"I know," Parker said. "Your kids are so cute." She was quiet for a few minutes, then she shook her head. "I can't stop thinking about the detective's daughter and the fact that she went missing around the same time as the others."

"Yeah, but if she was a problem child or just kind of restless and venturesome, he may be right— she just ran off, and her disappearance is unrelated to the others."

"Then why is he so interested in this case?" Parker asked.

"Good question."

Parker grinned. "That's my super power—coming up with good questions. Here we are," she said, parking in front of a modest house with a boarded-up window and a screen door dangling from one hinge.

"Do you think she'll mind that we have the cats with us?" Savannah asked.

"I don't know. We probably should have taken them back to the condo, but there just wasn't time. If there's a problem, we'll come back another time." Parker knocked on the door.

"Yes?" a large blond woman said, opening the door just a little.

"I'm Parker. I spoke with you on the phone earlier."

"Oh yes," the woman said. She picked up a small dog and opened the door wide, saying, "Oh, you have cats with you? Why do you have cats with you?"

"I'm sorry," Parker said. "If it's a problem, we…"

Before she could finish, Savannah spoke up. "We took our cats to visit a feral cat colony this morning, and they found a cat that needed surgery. We've been at the veterinary clinic and didn't have time to take these guys home. We'll hold them close. Will it be okay or…"

"Yeah," the woman said. She snuggled with the dog. "Gigi and I like cats, don't we, Poo-baby? Sure, come in. It's just odd to me to see cats on a leash, that's all. Our cat runs loose. Most of them do out here in this neck of the woods." She motioned with one arm. "Sit wherever you like."

"Thank you," Parker said, perching on a wingback chair. "By the way, this is Savannah and Rags. My cat's name is Olivia. What's your pooch's name? Oh, I heard you call her Gigi. And you're Mrs. Boehm?"

The woman nodded. "Dana. You said you want to hear the story of Kaylee's disappearance? I don't know anything about it, actually, only that she left home on January sixteenth and I've never seen or heard from her since."

"She left with her boyfriend?" Parker asked.

"I think so, but I can't be sure. She didn't tell me much about her life. We were kind of strangers living together." She chuckled. "You know, passing in the night." More seriously, she said, "I know that Kaylee wanted to get out on her own; she felt stifled here. When she met Ryan, an older kid with his own car and a job, I'm pretty sure she saw an opportunity to leave home, but she never spoke about it to me or to her father. She just left the house that night and—well, you know, disappeared."

"Did Kaylee take anything with her?" Savannah asked.

"Just her phone and her warmest jacket."
She added, "And her purse, of course. She carried a
great big purse, so she could have packed a change
of clothes, shoes—who knows what else?"

"So you expected her back that night?"
Parker asked.

"I sure did," Dana said. She frowned. "Well,
I did and I didn't. I always kinda knew she'd leave
someday, but I didn't expect it to be like that—with
no warning or goodbye or anything."

"What about Ryan? Did he go missing as
well?" Parker asked. "Did he ever get in touch with
his family after that night?"

"As far as I know they've never heard from
either Ryan or my daughter, but I can't say as I trust
what those people say all that much."

"Why's that?" Parker asked.

"Well, we come from different
neighborhoods and income brackets, if you know
what I mean. I don't think they liked their hoity-
toity college student dating a cute and flighty high
school senior who lives on this side of town. Get
my gist?" She looked down at the dog on her lap.
"They said a lot of things to my husband and me
that sounded like blame."

"You mean they blamed you for their son's
disappearance?" Parker asked.

Mrs. Boehm nodded. "Yes, in their mind my
little girl led their brilliant son down a forbidden

path. Yeah, I suspect that if they were to speak to their son, they probably wouldn't tell me about it."

"I'm sorry," Parker said.

"Thank you," Dana Boehm said. "So am I."

Savannah ran her hand over Rags's back and scratched his neck.

"Is he okay?" Mrs. Boehm asked.

"Yeah," Savannah said. "He just gets restless sometimes." She sat forward. "You know, when I was a girl I kept a diary. I think they call them journals now. Do you know if Kaylee kept one? Or maybe she kept notes from friends. When you went through her things did you find anything like that?"

The woman shook her head. "I sort of looked for something like that, but I didn't want to disturb her things just in case she came back. No, I didn't find anything. I spoke with her closest friends and neither of them seemed to think that Kaylee was planning to run away, with or without Ryan."

"Thank you, Mrs. Boehm," Parker said. "May I leave my card in case you think of something or find anything that might provide a clue as to what was in your daughter's mind that night?"

"Sure, but…"

"I know," Parker said, tenderly. "Just in case. Thank you for talking to us."

"Now where?" Savannah asked, as Parker drove on to the main highway.

"We have an appointment to talk to the couple whose part-time homeless son seems to be among the missing. I think they have an interesting story to tell."

"Did you get in touch with Ryan's family?" Savannah asked.

Parker shook her head. "The number is no longer in service. I thought we could do some research when we get a chance and maybe locate some current contact information for them."

"One forty-two," Savannah recited a little while later. "Gosh, that's a nice house. You wouldn't expect a child to live homeless if he had a place like that to come home to."

"Maybe they kicked him out," Parker said. She added, "Actually, that wasn't the vibe I got from his father. It sounds like the boy was welcome and even wanted at home." She turned the engine off, stepped out of the car, and led the way. "Let's go see what their deal is."

"Cats!" a woman squealed upon opening the door to them. "You brought cats? How fun. Are they therapy cats? I've seen therapy cats at the assisted living home where I volunteer."

Parker smiled. "Actually both of them do some therapy work. This is Olivia, and that handsome fellow is Ragsdale."

"How nice to meet you two," the woman said, petting Olivia, then Rags. She stood up. "I'm

Celeste." When a man entered the room she added, "This is Bob. Bob, look. They have therapy cats."

"How apropos," he said, smiling and greeting each of the cats. He looked at the two women. "So what can we do for you today? You said you have questions about Dustin? There always seem to be more questions about Dustin. Even *we* have unanswered questions. We just hope to heavens…" he started.

His wife glanced at him, then said, "Won't you ladies please come in and sit down? Can I get you something to drink?"

Parker shook her head. "By the way, I'm Parker and this is Savannah. As you know, we're interested in the occurrence seven years ago when your son may have disappeared with the others who went missing at the same time."

"Oh," Bob said, "are you one of those who believes they were taken by little green men to another planet?"

Parker chuckled. "No, sir. Not at all, but you must admit it's quite a mystery."

"Not so much," he said. "Dustin has always done his disappearing act—sometimes for a few days, once for an entire year."

"But never for seven years," Celeste said. "And the problem is we can't be sure when he actually disappeared—you know, if it was part of the disappearance of all those other young people, or…"

"As I understand it," Parker said, "they weren't all young people. There were a few older folks who went missing around that time. Some of them had irregular schedules like your son, so it's unclear if they disappeared that same night."

"And no catastrophe occurred that night that we know about," Bob said. "That was my theory—that they were all together, like in a plane or on a boat or at a house party even, when there was a crash, a sinking, or a kidnapping. Do you remember the kidnapping of the school children on that bus? The creep buried the bus with all those kids in there. Then there's the cult theory they all got caught up in a cult and were poisoned and buried or burned or..." his voice trailed off.

"Gosh, Bob," Savannah said, "you've really put a lot of thought into this, haven't you?"

"Wouldn't you if your child went missing?" he spat.

"Absolutely," Savannah said. "I'm sorry. I didn't mean to sound insensitive."

"It's okay," Celeste said. "You must forgive Bob. Anyone who has gone through something like this has to shoot off steam when we get the chance. The pain becomes too much to bear at times."

"I'm so sorry for what you've been through and are going through," Parker said. She paused, then asked more quietly, "So since that day you've had absolutely no contact with your son?"

"Actually, since five days before that

fateful time when so many were reported missing," Celeste said. "We've reached out to all of the other families we could locate, and even together we can't find a common denominator that would explain what happened." She choked up when saying, "I sometimes go into Dustin's room and just sit and pray and hope the answer will pop into my head so we'll know. A lot of things have come to me during those times, but I can't make myself believe the worst, and the happier thoughts never actually happen, so…"

Savannah smiled and asked tenderly, "Dustin still has a room here?"

Celeste nodded. "Yes, but he didn't—I mean, doesn't sleep there. He likes clean clothes. That's why he comes home every so often, for warm food and clean clothes. He leaves the dirties for me to wash and he takes a few of the clean ones with him. He doesn't sleep here very often, but when he does, he usually does so on the sly."

"What do you mean?" Parker asked.

"When we found out he was sleeping on a chaise lounge on the back deck, we put a bed in the garage for him. He tried to hide the fact that he used it fairly often, but I knew. I also left meals and sandwiches for him in the fridge out there. They disappeared pretty regularly." She frowned. "Not anymore. Not for about seven years, as a matter of fact. I left his bedroom just as it was when he launched out on his own, right after a couple of years of college."

"Yeah," Bob said, "something happened to him, and we don't know what it was—you know, to make him withdraw from life and live like a homeless person."

Celeste brightened. "Would you like to see his room?"

Savannah looked at Parker, and nodded. "Yes. We'd like that."

"This is nice," Parker said, glancing around the well-kept room." When Olivia reached up with her paws on Parker's leg, she petted her head and murmured, "Yes, I love you too, sweet thing."

Celeste and Savannah smiled at the calico.

"She's beautiful," Celeste said. She grinned. "What's she doing? It's like she's trying to get your attention or something."

"Cats like attention," Savannah said, "except when they don't."

Parker nodded. She kneeled next to Olivia. "What is it, girl?"

"How cute she is," Celeste said when Olivia put one paw on Parker's thigh.

Parker looked around and said, "I think she wants to show me something. Do you mind if I let her…?"

"By all means," Celeste said.

They watched as Olivia hopped up onto the bed and dug under a decorative pillow.

Parker apologized and picked up the cat. "No clawing, Olivia."

"Look," Savannah said, pointing. "She pulled something out from under there."

Celeste picked it up. "Oh yes. I found this in one of Dustin's pockets a year or so ago. I don't know why, but I tucked it under there."

"What is it?" Savannah asked.

Celeste waved it in the air. "Oh, an advertisement from a newspaper—you know, promotion. This one's for a local band. Dustin likes music."

Parker took the paper and read, "The Three Boy Band." She asked, "Do you know these young men?"

Celeste shook her head. "I've never heard of them. I just happened to finally get courage enough to look through some of Dustin's things, and…" she choked up again.

"I'm so sorry," Parker said. "It must be a nightmare for the two of you." No one spoke for a moment, then Parker picked up Olivia. "Well, we'll get out of your hair. Do let us know if you think of anything else." She asked. "Is it okay if I take a picture of this ad?"

"Take it for all we care," Bob said, joining the women in Dustin's room.

"No," Celeste said. "I don't think…"

Parker removed her phone and took a picture of the advertisement, saying, "No problem."

"Oh," Savannah moaned once they were in the car with the cats. "I feel so much pain for those parents. It would be awful to lose a child, but to not know what happened to him would add a whole different level of pain and stress."

"I know," Parker agreed. "Okay, let's go home and talk to the man whose daughter went missing after or while on a camping trip, shall we?"

The following morning Parker and Savannah sat together in the condo kitchen over breakfast.

"How's everything at home?" Parker asked.

"What?" Savannah muttered.

Parker smiled. "I heard you laughing in your room this morning. I figured you were touching base with your family."

"Yes," Savannah said. "Everyone's just fine. Yeah, Teddy was trying to tell me a story about helping his sister and his daddy feed the horses. Lily kept correcting him. I heard Michael in the background scolding Glori about something."

"Oh, your calico?" Parker asked. "What, pray tell, did that darling do?"

"I don't know, but it sure sounded like a chaotic moment—cats, a toddler, and a precocious five year old...oh my," Savannah said.

Parker grinned. "Glad to be out of the line of fire, huh?"

192

"Not really," Savannah said. "I miss my family. Thank heavens for Mom; she keeps things running fairly smoothly when the kids and the animals get the crazies."

"She lives there with you all?" Parker asked. "How long as she been there?"

"Since Lily was a baby," Savannah said. "That was one of the best decisions Michael and I have made since we decided to get married and have children. And Mom seems to be in her element."

Parker smiled. "In some ways I so envy you having a family, but I just can't bring myself to think about settling down yet."

"Who's settled down?" Savannah quipped.

"Touché," Parker said, grinning. "You do get out and about, and you do make a mean omelet. This is really good."

"Thank you. Glad you like it. Do you cook?" Savannah grinned, then said, "Oh, it seems like you told me once you're not much for cooking—something about an emu, right?"

"Yes. Wade calls me a clumsy emu in the kitchen, unless he's hungry and I'm the only other person around, then he'll sing my culinary praises."

Savannah laughed. "Fickle, is he?"

Parker nodded. "And self-serving, and an opportunist, and my idol—I love that guy to pieces." She leaned forward. "So what do you think about our FaceTime conversation with

Ed yesterday?" She winced. "Poor guy. He's so heartbroken and…"

"And broken," Savannah said. "Yeah, there are a lot of questions there—who did Kaci go camping with? He assumed friends, but he doesn't know who it might have been. None of her friends are missing, right?"

"Right," Parker said. "He doesn't know about a boyfriend. It doesn't sound like he and his daughter were very close, or…"

"Or he just doesn't remember."

"He seemed pretty clear about that night," Parker said. "Although he sure didn't have much information about Kaci's plans."

Savannah nodded. "Yeah, Kaci was evasive about the camping trip she was supposedly going on, and he let her be. He didn't question her. He said he was trying to give her more space—give her the illusion that he trusted her."

"Uh-huh," Parker muttered. "According to him, she left alone. He's pretty sure she took a small tent, but he doesn't know where she planned to camp. She left before dark, right?"

"Barely, from the sounds of it," Savannah said. "I'd sure like to get the transcripts of the interviews with these folks at the time of the disappearances."

"Yeah," Parker said. "I thought that's what the detective had given us. I wonder if he has them." She shrugged and looked at Savannah. "So

194

what do we know? Are we any closer to figuring out what happened?" Parker was quiet for a moment. "I'd like to know more about what was going on that week—in particular that night. Several people have told us it had rained a lot that week, but some remember it being clear that night."

"Right," Savannah said. "Do you think that's a clue?"

Parker shrugged again. "Could be, I guess." She reached for a stack of papers, shuffled through them, and said, "I've wondered about this other homeless guy—the one who wasn't officially considered missing until almost a year later. I don't know what made his family or the authorities decide he might have gone missing with all of the others that night."

"Because no one had seen him since before that happened," Savannah said.

"Yeah, I guess the reason he's included in this batch of missing persons is because he also appears to have disappeared without a trace."

"Well, we have a trace now," Savannah said, "at least it appears we do. I guess we'll know more about that once the authorities and families are told about all the items the detective has uncovered."

"You mean that the cats uncovered," Parker corrected.

"Do you think the feral cats dug up all that stuff?" Savannah asked.

Parker nodded. "I think they uncovered bits and pieces of it, and the detective has been finding more of it since he's been out there poking around." She picked up her chiming phone, announcing, "It's Flo. Good morning, Flo."

"Good morning," Flo said. "The detective wants to start digging at the colony, did you know that?"

"No," Parker said. "He didn't say anything to us about it."

"He's convinced that whatever happened all those years ago happened right there where the clothes and other things are showing up. He believes that the cats will remain safe. He wants to use only a shovel and only in that one area for now, so it shouldn't disturb the cats. They have quite a large area to roam, as you know. What do you two gals think?"

"It's probably a good idea. Let me run it by Savannah, who knows more about cat colonies than I do. Can I call you back? Actually, why don't you trot on over here and we can discuss it."

Flo arrived a few minutes later and was greeted by the fur brigade. "Hi, you two lovelies," she cooed. "Oh, you're such nice friendly cats." She said to the women, "This calico is so soft. I could pet her for hours." She scratched Rags's head affectionately. "And you are adorable. Quite the gentleman, aren't you?"

"Do you have cats?" Savannah asked.

"Not currently," Flo said. "I miss having one at home, but I'd like to leave a spot for one of the ferals if we can successfully socialize any from this group."

"Maybe you can adopt one of Selma's kittens," Savannah suggested. "They'll need homes in eight or ten weeks."

"How are they," Flo asked, "and how is Selma? Did she make it through the birthing?"

"Dr. Darling is pretty wonderful," Savannah said. "She did an excellent job, and Selma seemed willing to participate fully. She fought hard. I guess she wants to stick around to raise those adorable little ones."

"How many did we get?" Flo asked.

"Three," Savannah said. "The original three. We lost the last one, unfortunately."

"But surely we would have lost all of them," Parker said, running her hand over Olivia's fur, "if it wasn't for these two."

Flo smiled. "Talk about wonderful. Yeah, I wouldn't mind having a Ragdoll kitten." Just then, Olivia flopped over onto her side and rolled around a little. "Now that's a Ragdoll trait, right?"

"I think so," Parker said. She asked Savannah, "Does Rags do that?"

"Only in my lap," Savannah said. "He'll get in my lap and just flop like a dishrag and lie against me purring for a while, until he's ready to take off on his next adventure."

Flo smiled at Rags, then asked, "So how are things going with the detective's research?"

Parker glanced at Savannah and said, "Good. He did a good job of cluing us in, and we've been talking to the families of some of the missing people. What a trip. I sometimes wonder if the detective's spaceship theory has some merit. It's sure a puzzle what may have happened to all those people."

"When's he starting the digging?" Savannah asked. "You know, we could help with that. It might be interesting, and he could probably use the help."

"Yeah, I agree," Parker said. "Is he there now?"

Flo shrugged. "I'm not sure. I just know he was going over there sometime today."

"I'll call him," Savannah suggested.

"Good," Parker agreed. She said to Flo, "I think it's probably important for us to move forward on your fundraising and donor issue while Savannah's here."

"We're on *your* schedule," Flo said. "You're calling the shots."

"Did you hear that?" Parker asked, when she saw Savannah pocket her phone.

Savannah looked at her. "What?"

"Flo said they're ready to move forward with the fundraising projects—you know, the ideas you have for them. When is the detective going out to the site?"

"He's there now," Savannah said.

Parker stood up. "Why don't we go help him? Oh!" she yelped. "What about shovels?" She grinned. "You didn't happen to pack one of your horse pooper-scooper shovels in your car did you?"

Savannah grinned. "No, but he has extras. I guess he knew we might come through."

Parker turned to Flo, "Can you get a core group together this afternoon, say around three?"

Flo nodded. "I'm sure I can. Want to meet at Alma's?"

"We could meet here," Savannah said. "I think it would be a good idea to meet with a smaller group to start with. It's been my experience..."

"I get it," Flo said. "Oh yes, you get too many women together and nothing gets done; there's too much chatter and not enough decision-making. Let me call, like you said, the core group, and we'll meet you back here at three."

Savannah nodded. She moved closer to Flo. "And be thinking about some of your local companies, especially those that have a business related to animals or have a heart for animals—a feed-store chain or pet-food processing plant, a veterinary association, for example. Let's try to come up with a list of those who might be able to donate the funds or something of value to your group."

"Something of value?" Flo repeated. "Like what?"

"Oh, a billboard where you can promote your cause, an item the group can sell..." Savannah grinned, "...land where the cats can live safely. Do you have a body of officers?"

"Yes," Flo said. We're a 501(c)(3). That was established years ago, and we've done everything we can to protect it."

"Great!" Savannah said. "I'd say you're on your way to accomplishing your goals for the cats. With Parker writing your story, you'll bring in even more funds." She faced Parker. "You *are* going to write about them, right?"

"Yes," she said. "I know you can't stay long, so I want to accomplish the things we need you and Rags for first. Once you go back to *your* reality— you know husband, kids," Parker said, grinning, "then I'll start the interviews with some of the old-timers in this group. I've been taking pictures and making notes behind the scenes."

"Really?" Savannah said. "So that's why I hear you behind me sometimes—you're making voice memos on your phone?"

Parker grinned.

"See you at three," Flo said, preparing to leave. "Good luck with your digging. I was out there this morning, and most of the cats were south of where the detective wants to dig, so I think they'll be out of the way." She asked, "Will you take your cats?"

"Yeah, cats can dig, right?" Parker quipped.

Savannah thought for a moment. "I guess we could. Those two do know how to sniff out things that don't belong."

"That don't belong?" Flo repeated.

"Well, just last week," Parker said, "they dug up a bunch of jewelry that another cat had stolen and buried."

"What?" Flo shrieked.

"We'll tell you about it later," Savannah said. "I think we should get out there and help the detective."

"And see what we can find," Parker said.

"Ahoy, there Detective!" Parker called when she and Savannah arrived at the colony site.

"Ahoy?" he repeated, laughing. "That's rather nautical of you."

"So how's it going?" Savannah asked, walking closer with Rags.

"Dismally," he said.

"Why?" she asked quietly.

He leaned on his shovel and swiped at his forehead with his shirtsleeve, then nodded to his right.

Parker and Savannah walked closer to where he had meticulously placed a variety of items on a tarp spread across the ground. "Oh," Savannah groaned, "someone's purse." She started to pick it up, then changed her mind. She saw the detective watching her and asked, "Do you know who…?"

He bowed his head and said quietly, "It's my daughter's."

Parker squeezed her eyes shut for a moment. "Damn!"

Savannah blew out a breath in frustration and gently squeezed Jud's arm. "I'm so sorry."

"It is what it is," he said dismissively, jamming his shovel forcefully into the dirt.

Parker grimaced, then quietly scoured the items on the tarp, finally asking, "What's this?"

Jud looked up. He cleared his throat. "I'd say it's a piece from a musical instrument— probably a guitar."

"Oh," was all Parker could manage. She stood up and looked around. "But how…"

"Yes, how did all this stuff end up here?" he asked.

"And why isn't there a common denominator to connect all of these people?" Savannah mumbled.

"There probably is," Parker reasoned. "We just don't know what it is." She turned to the detective. "What's your best guess—I mean, your educated guess from your experience in law enforcement? How do you think all of those

202

people's belongings got buried out here? Where are the missing people?"

He looked at her, then at Savannah, and finally said, "Come on, I want to show you something else." He led the two women to his car, opened the trunk, and pointed.

"It's a box of bones," Savannah said, leaning in.

Parker took one look and backed away.

"I've been collecting them pretty near every time I come out here," he said solemnly.

"So there goes your spaceship theory," Parker muttered.

"A mass murderer?" Savannah suggested. "A massacre."

"Possibly," Jud said.

"Is that your best guess?" Parker asked.

He shook his head. "Either something like that or a catastrophic event."

"One that would leave no evidence for seven solid years?" Parker asked. Feeling somewhat overwhelmed, and more eager than ever to find the answers, she said. "Hey, give me a shovel. Let's go to work."

The trio had been digging for a couple of hours, dredging up bits and pieces of clothing, footwear, parts of documents, even jewelry when the detective took a break. He leaned on his shovel and gazed at the items they'd carefully laid out on the tarp. "What do you say we call it a day?" he suggested. "I've probably actually got enough things here to piece the whole story together—all I need is commentary from those families."

"You're going to tell them about this?" Savannah asked.

He shook his head. "No. Not right away. I don't want to create pandemonium for the cats and all those nice ladies."

No one spoke for a few moments when Savannah said, "Hey, I've been thinking. I may be off base, but I can't shake the image."

"Image?" Parker questioned.

"Could there be an underground cave or tunnel out here?" she blurted. She squinted in thought. "...an underground passageway, an abandoned mine, where those people met for some reason and died of asphyxiation or..."

"Maybe there was an explosion," Parker suggested.

"Underground?" Jud questioned. "What would bring that group of people all together in a place like that?"

"Drugs," Parker suggested.

"Porn," Savannah said. When the others looked at her she quipped, "Ever hear of underground movies?"

"Hey, that's almost funny," Parker said, not laughing.

The detective frowned. "I'd hoped this was simply a dumping ground. You know how people will haul their trash to a remote spot and dump it."

Parker sighed deeply. "Well, back to the drawing board with our interviews." She asked, "Detective, do you think you could get us more detailed information about the interviews done seven years ago? If we could get our hands on those transcripts it might help us to ask more relevant questions when we meet with the families."

"Makes sense," Jud said. "In fact, I've been thinking it's time we let the police in on our little secret," he chuckled, "whether they want in or not."

"What?" Savannah said.

"Yeah, will they really want to come out here and revisit a cold case this old?" Parker asked. She tilted her head. "They don't even know what exists out here do they? No one but us knows about what you've found do they?"

"Exactly," the detective said. "But I'm weary, and I'm getting too emotional about what I'm finding. I think I need to back off." He asked, "Ms. Campbell, do you know anyone on the force here?"

"I probably do," she said. "I've worked with some officers and a captain here on cases."

"Captain Dennison?"

"Yes," she said. "Angelo Dennison."

"Well, I think I'll give him a call as soon as I get this load to my barn. I'll let him know you're here and involved. He'll either..." Jud started.

She smiled. "I think he'll welcome my involvement. We were quite compatible on the last case we worked together."

"Parker," Savannah said, nudging her. "What's your pretty girl doing?"

"Oh," she yelped. "Olivia, don't you dare chew through that leash. I don't have an extra one with me."

"She chews through her leashes?" Savannah asked, amused.

"Well, she tries to," Parker said, trotting to where Olivia sat. She released the tied end of the leash and asked, "Is there something you want to show us, girl?"

They all watched as the tri-color cat pulled against her leash. When Savannah saw Rags tugging at his restraint, she released him, and the women trotted after the two cats, who both ran in the same direction.

"What are they up to?" Jud asked, trailing along.

The cats slowed down when they reached the edge of the trees and sniffed the air, each tilting their head. Without warning, Olivia leaped forward, pulling Parker off balance.

"Do I hear running water?" Savannah asked, trying to keep up with Rags and Olivia.

"Probably," Judson said. "There used to be a river running through here. I thought it dried up, but maybe it just changed course. Waterways will do that."

"Oh, there it is," Parker said, pointing. "Yes, water." She picked up Olivia. "You and your water fetish."

"She's a water witch?" Jud asked.

Parker nodded. "You might say that." She giggled. "You should have seen the bathroom at the Malibu Police Station after Olivia trashed it last week. Water everywhere."

"What was she doing at the police station, for heaven's sake?" Savannah asked.

"She got arrested," Parker answered, matter-of-factly. "Then she escaped from the pen they put her in and turned from terrorist to therapy cat for an abused child."

Savannah stared down at Olivia and shook her head. "And I thought Rags was out of control." She picked up her grey-and-white cat. "Well, if we're finished digging for the day, we'd better take you home. We have a meeting pretty soon." She stopped and asked, "But Detective, what about the cats? If you start bringing police in here and digging machinery and all that, it will disturb the cats and pretty much ruin all the work the ladies have done out here to keep them safe."

"I know," he said. "I'm awfully sorry about that, but I don't know if it can be helped."

Savannah stared at him for a moment and asked, "Can you give us time?"

"How much time?" he asked.

Savannah looked at Parker. "What do you think?"

Parker looked around the area, then said, "Hey, I have an idea. Detective, where do you propose they start the digging?"

"I don't know how far and wide they'll want to go. Maybe as far as where you see those tallest trees down there."

"Can you set that in concrete for us?" Parker asked.

"What?" he asked.

"Can we keep the equipment and people, say, on this side of that pile of rocks at least for the next few days or so?"

"I can sure try, and with you working with us, Ms. Campbell, there's more likelihood of that."

"What's your idea?" Savannah asked. "How would we keep the cats over there?"

Parker smiled. "Fencing. Some of that nice tall, sturdy fencing like is at the Ragsdale Cat Ranch. I happen to know that the ladies have a bank account. Let's see if they can afford that fencing around this area as a temporary measure. If they purchase the fencing they can store it and use it again should they need it—you know, like for a permanent enclosure."

"Yes," Savannah said. "If they could fence that entire area, it would be large enough to keep the cats happy and small enough to keep them safe. Brilliant! Good thinking, Parker. Yes, let's present the idea to the ladies. So you think we could get it constructed in two day's time?"

"We'll make it happen." Parker picked up Olivia and the group traipsed back to their cars. "I'll be in touch," she said to the detective.

"Great. I'll hold off saying anything to anyone until I get the go-ahead from you ladies."

"Thanks," Parker said. "You're a gem." She put Olivia in the car, turned back, and asked, "May I hug you?"

"By all means," Jud said, embracing her.

"I'm so sorry," she murmured.

"About what?" he asked, pulling away.

"Well, what you're going through and, you know, discovering evidence that your daughter..."

"You mean because I found her purse out here? Don't mean nothing," he said, shaking it off. "It could be that someone stole it and ran with it into that underground cave you girls mentioned." He got into his car and drove away.

Chapter Seven

"What's your take on the plan?" Savannah asked later that evening as the two women mulled over the events of the day. "Do you think it can be accomplished?"

"Sure, as long as the detective holds off on getting the police involved until that fence is up. Flo has a company lined up to start on that tomorrow," Parker said. She shook her head. "Those poor cats. They've lived in relative peace out there for so long, and now they'll be disturbed by those fencing people, then the sound of heavy equipment."

"Yeah, it's just too bad they couldn't have been moved before all of this came to a head," Savannah said. "Poor timing." She was quiet for a moment, then said, "I wonder if the cats know what happened there."

"What?"

"Well, they were there when whatever happened occurred. They may have been the only eye witnesses."

Both women were quiet for a few moments, then Parker sat up straighter. "Were they? I mean, if the cats were there, that means the ladies were feeding them. I wonder what they saw or noticed that would shed some light on what happened back then. Did we even ask Flo or Alma or Peggy that question?"

"No," Savannah said. "I don't think we did. Yes, they might have noticed something and didn't think it was important enough to tell anyone. What time is it? Is it too late to call Flo?" She chuckled. "She's probably tired of us by now, especially after that three-hour meeting here this afternoon."

Parker smiled. "I think it went well, don't you?"

"Excellent," Savannah agreed. "We were able to share a lot of ideas and perspective related to fundraising. And once we started laying out ideas for them, they really began to conceptualize what it's going to take, don't you think so?"

"I do," Parker said. "It's refreshing working with a group of such savvy women." She stood up. "Let me see if Flo's still up." She peered out the patio door and reported, "Her lights are on. I'll call and see if we can get her and some of the others to be thinking about what they may have noticed at the colony site seven years ago around January sixteenth. She picked up her phone, but before she could place a call, it chimed. She jumped a little and chuckled. "It's Flo. Hello Flo. How are you?" She walked into the kitchen, returning several minutes later to find Savannah curled up on the loveseat with Rags and Olivia. Parker smiled.

"Olivia is such a love bug," Savannah said, petting her. When Rags pawed at her hand she chuckled and ruffled the fur around his neck. "Yes, Ragsie, I love you, too." She looked at Parker. "What did Flo want? Did you ask her about what she remembers?"

Parker nodded. "She said she doesn't remember anything about that week. She believes that's about the time she had shoulder surgery, and she wasn't going out there then. She doesn't remember hearing about anything odd happening, but she'll ask around." Parker stared down at her phone for a moment and said, do you suppose..."

"What?" Savannah asked.

"Wade," Parker said. "Wade can do telepathy with cats. He admittedly can't tune into cats as easily from a distance, but..."

"Oh my gosh," Savannah said. "Let's give it a try. I mean, there are a lot of cats. Maybe if he could tap into the collective mind out there..."

"Great idea!" Parker said. "I'll call him right now."

"Tell him 'hi' for me," Savannah said. When Parker finished a lively conversation with her brother, Savannah asked, "Well? What did he say?"

Parker smiled. "He said to tell you hi. He also sent a hug. He was excited about our case."

"Our case, huh?" Savannah repeated, laughing.

"Well, we're sure involved," Parker reminded her. "He said he would see what he can get from the cats, but he did have one vision while we were talking."

"What?" Savannah asked eagerly.

"Mud," Parker said.

Savannah wrinkled up her nose. "Mud? What about mud? I mean, there sure is mud out at the colony site. I was glad to see that today. It made for easier digging."

"Yes, it's kind of silt-like, isn't it?"

"He also saw rain, a lot of rain," Parker said. You may remember that someone said it rained a lot that week. Do you think…"

"What?" Savannah asked. She laughed. "That all that stuff fell out of the sky? Clothes, purses, shoes, and jewelry rained down over the cat colony?" She frowned. "From where?"

Instead of answer, Parker asked, "How would you like to go on a hike tomorrow?"

"A hike? Weren't we going to meet with a few of the ladies again in the morning?"

"That's why Flo called," Parker said. "She changed our meeting time. She wants to be at the job site to make sure the fence gets installed and that it's going to serve the purpose and all. She rescheduled the meeting until late tomorrow. What do you think —about a hike, I mean?"

"Sure, I guess," Savannah agreed. "Why?"

Parker grinned. "I have a hunch."

"Oh?" Savannah questioned. "About the missing people?"

Parker nodded.

Just then Olivia rolled over onto her back next to Savannah and looked up at her. Savannah giggled. "Is that an invitation to pet your fluffy tummy?"

"I wouldn't if I were you," Parker warned.

"She doesn't appreciate a tummy rub, huh?" Savannah asked.

"No. I don't know what happened to her that makes her so touchy on the tummy, but even though she does that inviting rollover, no, that is not an invitation to touch the tummy."

Savannah ran her fingers over Olivia's head and neck and the cat began to purr. "You are just so cute," she crooned. She looked at Parker. "Tell me how you acquired this interesting fur-baby. We've started to talk about her beginnings a couple of times, and we always get sidetracked."

"I've noticed that," Parker said. She smiled at Olivia. "Well, I was between cats. My Mr. Wonderful, Beans, had crossed over the rainbow bridge, and I wasn't sure I wanted another cat."

"But Olivia changed your mind?"

"Something like that," Parker said.

"Did Beans travel with you and everything?"

"He did occasionally, but he wasn't involved in my work the way Olivia is. He had his place in my heart and at my hearth, but he wasn't all that outgoing, and he had little sense of adventure. He didn't appreciate new experiences. I left him home with a sitter more often than I took him with me. My lifestyle wasn't actually conducive to having a cat, or so I thought. I always felt bad leaving Beans, and I didn't think it would be fair to adopt again after he died when I'm gone so much."

"And then you met Olivia," Savannah said, smiling down at the calico.

"And then I met Olivia," Parker confirmed. "The poor little thing was evidently born under a house—either that, or she strayed from her mother and ended up living under a house down in the LA area. That's as far back as I can trace her beginnings, and I got that far only through word of mouth." She chuckled. "And my over-the-top sense of curiosity."

"How old was she when she was discovered under the house?" Savannah asked.

"Around eight or ten weeks, as near as I can figure," Parker said. "I didn't meet her until she was six months old. She'd been through a lot by then."

"Oh?" Savannah asked, frowning.

"Yeah, the homeowner trapped the scruffy little thing and took her to a shelter. Olivia escaped, slipped out of the facility, and found her way to a nearby colony." She shook her head. "I mean, how gutsy is that for such a little pipsqueak to walk into a cat colony and make herself at home?"

Savannah frowned. "She probably had to earn her place there—you know, by challenging the other cats or by being challenged, unless there happened to be a gentle surrogate cat that took her under his paw. Sometimes that happens."

"It's hard to know how that went down, but the colony was near a housing tract, and Olivia and another cat—maybe that surrogate you mentioned—well, they showed up at a kind cat-lover's home and the kind cat-lover began feeding them. However, when other cats became aware of the buffet being served there the kind cat-lover complained to her grown son, who thought that a good way to resolve the matter was to trap as many of the cats as he could, including Olivia, and haul them to an industrial area where cats were known to gather. He figured the cats would be welcome there and earn their keep as mousers; industrial areas always need mousers. But by then there were dozens of cats and kittens, as you can imagine."

"Poor thing," Savannah muttered. "And she was still a kitten?"

Parker nodded. "Yes, I think she landed there when she was around four months old. So the cats became a problem at the industrial site and the surrounding homes, and they began to get publicity—evidently negative publicity. Well, I was on assignment at one of the businesses in the industrial park a few months later."

"Because of the cat situation?" Savannah asked.

"No," Parker said. "It was a case of too many employees getting hurt on the job—or claiming they were hurt on the job—and collecting disability. The government was on it, but one of my editors wanted the story, so she sent me out there. As the saying goes, one thing led to another, and I became aware of the cat problem. With the manager's blessings, I got involved in relocating those cats, leaving just a few as mousers."

"By yourself?" Savannah asked.

"No, I called in some of the local TNR people and they took over the actual work."

Savannah smiled. "And that's when you met Olivia?"

"Not right away," Parker said. "I first laid eyes on her one day when I was eating my lunch. I'd been conducting interviews all morning, and the last one spilled over into my usual lunch hour. I had just a few minutes to eat before my next interview, so I bought a sandwich and chips from a vending machine and sat out back to eat and relax a bit. I'd just about finished eating, and I was thinking about my next interview when I saw something out of the corner of my eye. I was pretty sure it was one of the cats—we'd caught most of them by then. The volunteers had their sights on two large toms and I was watching for them whenever I had the chance. They'd be going to the vet for a snip-snip, then off to a cat colony several miles away. I'd hoped to see one of them that afternoon, but no. What emerged from under the shrub was something very different from the scruffy cats we'd been dealing with. This was a small, underweight calico. She was dirty, but still fluffy and just about the most adorable half-grown kitten you can imagine. At least she sure caught my eye."

"I *can* imagine," Savannah said.

"She just sat down as confident as you please and stared at me," Parker said.

"And what did you do?" Savannah asked, amused.

"I stared back. They'd stopped feeding the cats, hoping they'd go into the traps, so I knew she was hungry. I dug out a piece of turkey from my yucky vending-machine sandwich and tossed it to her. She strutted toward it, keeping an eye on me, her beautiful fluffy tail standing up like a flag, and she inhaled that bite. So I reached into my backpack and pulled out some kibbles."

Savannah chuckled. "You carried kibbles with you?"

Parker nodded. "I still do." She continued, "The ragamuffin kitten ate those. I had to get to my next appointment, so I excused myself and left. The last I saw, the kitten scurried back into the shrubbery, but I couldn't get her out of my mind.

Late that day I finished my work and went back out to where I'd seen the spunky little calico. I put my backpack down and walked around the area trying to find her, but she was nowhere to be seen. It was getting dark, I was tired, so I gave up and returned to where I'd left my things." She smiled. "That's when I saw her. She was curled up sound asleep on my pack. I was surprised when she let me pick her up. I slipped her inside my jacket where it was warm and took her home. We've been together ever since."

"What, two years, you said?"

Parker nodded.

"What possessed you to start traveling with her?" Savannah asked.

"That's easy," Parker said. "The truth is, I couldn't bear to leave her. She bonded so quickly and completely with me that I just couldn't leave her. It was either quit my work and stay with her or take her with me. That's when I discovered how really adaptable she is, and even helpful in the work I do. It's as if she was bred and trained to be my assistant."

Savannah smoothed Olivia's cheek. "That's quite a story, Olivia. You are one very special kitty, you know it?" She asked, "So how did you find out about her beginnings? It seems as though a path such as Olivia traveled would be hard or impossible to track."

"True," Parker said, "but I was so curious about what might have contributed to her personality and traits that I simply traced her paw prints as best I could. I actually happened across the young man who dumped her at the industrial park. That was a fluke. He worked there in one of the businesses. I had to make a couple more trips out there to talk to people, and after cleaning Olivia up and fitting her with a harness and leash, which she took to immediately, I took her out there with me. This man saw her and asked about her. That's when I learned how she came to be at this place. From there I discovered the location of nearby colonies and found out who managed them. It's all about searching for leads and following them." She chuckled. "It also means doing stakeouts and being very, very patient. Eventually I met some of the caretakers of one of the colonies, and they told me a little about a small, but gutsy, calico they'd seen a time or two chowing down with some of the bigger cats."

"You're good," Savannah complimented. She picked up Olivia and snuggled with her. "And you are one lucky, lucky kitty, although it sounds like you may have manipulated the situation a bit there."

"Do you think?" Parker said, grinning. "Oh, and people ask how she got her name."

"Yes, how did you happen to give her such a noble name? Where did that come from?" Savannah laughed. "It's a far cry from Mr. Rags's rag-tag name."

"For sure," Parker said, also laughing. She then revealed, "Actually, Olivia named herself."

"What?" Savannah squealed.

Parker grinned. "Yes, I'd been struggling to come up with just the right name." When Savannah laughed, she looked at her.

"Sorry," Savannah said, attempting to contain herself. "I was just thinking about the name you gave your other cat. Beans. What's up with that name?"

"Oh, that was just a silly play on his toes. They're sometimes referred to as beans. His were particularly cute—brown instead of pink…"

"So you named him after his own toes?" Savannah asked.

Parker nodded. "Something like that, but I thought Olivia should have a more queenly name, and I guess so did she, because one day she showed me something and it clicked."

"What, for heaven's sake?" Savannah asked eagerly.

Parker put her hands up and bounced in her chair gleefully. "Okay, it may sound a bit weird, but here's how it happened, cross my heart…"

"And Olivia is crossing her paws," Savannah said, pointing at the calico. She does that a lot, doesn't she?"

Parker nodded. "Yes, it's her trademark pose—that and the neat stretch where she arches her tail over her back."

"Interesting," Savannah said. "Okay, let's hear how she picked out her own name."

"I was shopping online for a book to give a friend's little girl for her birthday," Parker started. "I was invited to this gala event that the three-year-old would probably sleep through. It sounded fun, and I wanted to choose a meaningful gift—you know, something educational. I started scrolling through children's books, when all of a sudden, Olivia, the yet-unnamed kitten, leaped up onto the couch with me. I could tell she'd just had a drink from her fountain—her little face was wet. Well, something on my laptop caught her attention and she moved closer. Before I could get my hands on her, she sniffed the screen and left a nose print smack-dab in the middle of one of the Olivia the Pig books. I looked at her and she looked at me and I said, 'That's it. You're Olivia.' End of story."

Savannah applauded. "I love that story, but it's certainly not the end." She ruffled Olivia's fur again. "Is it, pretty girl? There are a lot of chapters ahead to your beautiful story. She yawned. "Well, Ragsie, shall we get ready for bed?"

Both women laughed when Rags leaped down from the loveseat and turned in circles.

"He's excited about going to bed?" Parker asked.

"He's excited about his bedtime snack," Savannah explained.

"Oh, that *is* exciting." Parker stood up. "Well, night-night, everyone. See you in the morning."

"Yeah, so where are we going hiking?" Savannah asked. "Where will your hunch take us?"

"I'm not exactly sure," Parker said. When her phone chimed, she answered it. "Hello, Detective. Oh, yes, I think that will work—see you around seven thirty, then. We'll put the coffee on."

"Seven thirty?" Savannah repeated. "In the morning? Why?"

"Apparently he has a hunch too."

"I have a theory," Detective Caldwell said over coffee the following morning, "and I'd like to run it by you ladies."

"A mass grave?" Parker asked.

"Yes," he agreed. "A mass murder, perhaps, that most likely happened somewhere else by someone who has access to heavy equipment and is familiar with that type of machinery."

"So you think those poor people were killed somewhere else and their bodies and belongings were moved to that spot and buried there?" Parker asked.

"It's possible," Jud Caldwell insisted. "Years of erosion and rain have caused a sort of regurgitation of the soil, like ground will do with rocks sometimes." He looked at the women. "Have you ever lived someplace where rocks just seem to appear overnight? It happens."

"A graveyard, huh?" Savannah muttered. "So you think there's a mass murderer roaming the streets? That's spooky."

"Everything about this case is spooky," Parker said.

The detective leaned toward the women. "I'm thinking about bringing in a backhoe."

"So, have you decided to involve the police?" When he shook his head, she asked, "Won't people become suspicious if they see something that big going on out there?"

The detective choked up. "I have to know. It's tearing me up wondering—not knowing what happened."

"You're talking about your own daughter now, aren't you?" Savannah asked tenderly.

"I want to know if she's still alive. If not, I need to know she didn't suffer," he explained.

The trio sat quietly for a few moments, each with their own thoughts, then Savannah asked, "What are you looking for? What do you expect to find?"

"Answers!" he spat.

"Over and above what you've already found?" she asked. "Won't DNA testing give you at least some of the answers you want?"

"Maybe and maybe not," the detective said.

"When?" Parker asked.

"The backhoe is coming this morning."

"No," Savannah said. "Can't it wait one more day? They're installing the fencing today. Please, just give them one more day, for the cats' sake."

"Also," Parker said, "Savannah and I have something we want to check out this morning."

"What?" he asked suspiciously.

She hesitated, then said, "After the cats showed us the flow of water coming through that area, I got to thinking…"

"What?" he demanded.

"I'll tell you more about it once we've had a chance to check it out," Parker promised. When he stared at her over the rim of his coffee cup, she said, "It's a hunch— something that's been niggling at me. I want to check it out. Please give us just this one day."

"Okay," the detective said, grudgingly. He let out a long sigh. "What's one more day, right?"

Minutes later, the two women sat in the car, each with her own thoughts, as Parker drove up a winding mountain road. Savannah said, "I feel so sorry for the detective and the rest of those families. They seem to be holding out hope that their loved ones will return by some miracle."

"And you don't think they will?" Parker asked.

Savannah shook her head. "Do you? I mean, this week we seem to be uncovering evidence of the exact opposite—signs of a cataclysmic event or tragedy that apparently no one survived."

Parker nodded. "Yes, and that's important too." When Savannah looked at her she explained, "Those families need closure. If their loved ones are gone, they need to know what happened to them. They're all stuck in a sort of nowhere land. They need answers. I have to wonder how they've managed all these years not knowing."

"I agree," Savannah said. "I can't imagine how healing can take place without answers." She looked out the windows and asked, "Now where are we going?" She tried to steady herself in the seat. "This road is awful. Are you sure it's a road?"

"Yeah, it's like it's been abandoned." Parker motioned with her head. "Did you see that fence back there? I'm pretty sure someone cut it to allow access. It appears that the property owner or the county had the road blocked off."

"I can see why," Savannah said. "It's a terrible road." She yelped, "Oh look, a landslide. Yeah, no wonder they had that fence up. You wouldn't want to drive up here at night—the road is gone—just gone." When Parker turned off the car engine, Savannah asked, "So, where are we? Is this where you want to go hiking? Why?"

"Yes," Parker said. "I'm pretty sure this is where we'll find some of those answers—you know, for the families of the missing people."

"Oh?" Savannah said. "So where are we, exactly?"

"North of the cat colony."

Savannah looked around. "We are? Are you sure?"

"I'm pretty sure," Parker said. "Come on, let's take a walk."

"Walk where?" Savannah asked. "A big chunk of that road's gone. I don't see a trail."

"No, I don't think we'll find a trail. Come on," Parker said, trudging across the face of the mountain just above where the road had been. After a few minutes, she pointed. "Hey, there's a deer trail. Let's follow it. That'll make walking a little easier."

"Oh good," Savannah said later, pointing, "there's a road. Hey, it looks like the continuation of that bumpy road we came in on. Sheesh, I wonder what happened here."

"A landslide," Parker said, "or a mudslide. A whole wide section of this hillside has eroded or just flowed away."

"Sure looks that way," Savannah agreed, taking a swig from her water bottle. She looked around again. "Hey, you're right. We're smack-dab above the cat colony, aren't we?"

Parker nodded. "We sure are. Do you suppose…"

Oh," Savannah moaned. "Parker, are you saying… Yeah, someone told us it rained a lot the week all those people vanished."

"Yes," Parker affirmed, "and that rain could have undermined the hillside and sent it sliding down, down, down, down, right into that area of trees where the cats live."

Savannah suddenly felt a little sick. She asked, "So do you think all of those things the detective has found came from up here?"

Parker grimaced. "The evidence is certainly leaning in that direction."

Savannah looked around, finally saying, "Oh my gosh. If anyone was up here at that time…but why? Who would come up here at night, especially such a diverse group of people?"

"For the peace and quiet," Parker suggested. "Young people like to get away from adults and the authorities when they're smoking dope or drinking or whatever. You know that."

Savannah grinned. "Well, I didn't smoke dope, although I do know what you mean, but other than the solitude there doesn't seem to be much to attract someone up here." After considering this, she asked, "Do you think it was inviting before the slide—you know, with trees, picnic benches, fire pits? Now there's virtually no access and certainly nothing appealing about it."

Parker gazed into the distance. "That's a nice view of the city down there. Imagine it at night—the twinkling lights and all. It probably wasn't too uncommon for people to come up here and enjoy a pretty sunset at dusk and that city view at night."

"Oh," Savannah said grimly. "Oh my gosh. Do you think this is where it happened?"

"I'm pretty sure it did," Parker said, pulling out her phone and taking a few pictures. She faced Savannah. "But how did they get up here? Where are their cars? Did any of the parents say anything about their child's transportation that night?"

Savannah thought for a moment. "I read in some of that information the detective gave us that they found Kaci Stuart's car in a mini-mart parking lot a couple of days after she was reported missing."

"Interesting," Parker said. "So she probably hitched a ride, but some of them had to drive up here. Where are their cars?"

"Maybe the answer is in some of the police reports we haven't seen yet," Savannah suggested.

Parker gazed out toward the cat colony. "Or the answers are down there, buried with all that other stuff." She shook her head in exasperation. "Let's go down and see how the fence is coming along, shall we? Then we'd better have another talk with the detective."

"Drats," Savannah said. "I don't look forward to that—although I know he wants closure. He needs closure."

"Three-point-five miles," Parker said, pulling her car alongside the cat colony minutes later, "and probably half or three quarters of a mile as the crow flies." The two women got out of the car and watched as several men worked to install the fencing.

"Looks good," Savannah said. "They've gotten pretty far already this morning."

"Great. I know the detective is eager to move forward." Parker glanced up. "Here comes Peggy in her catmobile." She waved without much enthusiasm.

"Hi," Peggy called. "I saw you pull in. Did you come out to see the new fence? Looks good, doesn't it? It should serve its purpose while we need it."

"Yes," Savannah said. "How fortunate that the fencing people could come out on such short notice."

Peggy grinned. "It helps to know people, I can tell you that." She then said, "You ladies seem to lack your usual luster this morning. Is everything okay?"

Parker grimaced. "Yeah, well, I think the impact of what may have happened out here is starting to sink in, is all."

"So do you know what happened?" Peggy asked. "Have they found anything significant out here?"

Savannah patted Peggy's arm and fibbed. "Not yet. They should know more in a few days, don't you think so, Parker?"

Parker nodded, then asked more brightly, "Peggy, how are Selma and the kittens?"

"Wonderful," Peggy said, clasping her hands under her chin. "I'm having so much fun, and Selma seems happy to be home. She loves those babies—she's such a great mom." She reached for her phone and scrolled to find photos, which she showed to them.

Parker smiled. "Oh, they look great. Gosh, Selma looks like a new cat. All she needs is a little weight on those ribs."

She passed the phone to Savannah, who crooned, "Awww, beautiful. And those babies," she squealed, "they're adorable."

"You know, I was thinking," Parker said, "based on what they've been finding here in the colony, and what they could dig up here going forward, it's possible that developers will stand clear of this land. Know what I mean?"

"Yes," Savannah said. "Maybe it could be designated a sacred place, and the cats could continue living here."

"Although it would surely become a place of curiosity," Parker said. "People might come to remember, and inadvertently disturb the cats."

"Do you think it's a burial ground?" Peggy asked quietly. "I hate, hate, hate thinking that the cats might have been witness to a horrible act of violence."

"I doubt it," Parker said. "It's looking more like a natural disaster."

"What," Peggy asked, alarmed, "a cave-in, a sinkhole or a-a-a, what's it called— quicksand? Is there quicksand out there?"

Parker shook her head. "I don't think so." She then asked, "Hey, Peggy, do you remember the week when those people went missing? Someone said it had rained a lot. Did anything change out here in the colony that week—in particular, after it stopped raining?"

Peggy took a deep breath and blew it out. "Not that I recall. I just remember it was muddy as all get-out. I know that because I had cat duty that week, if I'm remembering right. It was pretty tense here in the community because of the missing people, so I was preoccupied, but I do remember having to wear my rubber boots out here. Oh yes, I had to go home and get them because I couldn't find the cats' food and water bowls. That's the week those bowls went missing. I mean they were gone. We finally recovered one a year or so later. It was broken. That's right, we never found the others. That was a mystery."

"So the bowls disappeared and it was muddy?" Parker asked.

"Yes, sloshy, sloppy mud like we'd never seen before. It took a long while to dry up out there because of the shade from the trees, but it finally did, and we were back to normal," Peggy said.

"Were the cats all accounted for?" Savannah asked.

"What?" Peggy questioned.

"Were all the cats okay after that rain and mud and all?"

"Oh yes, I believe so. There were a few weeks when we didn't traipse out there very far, as you can imagine, especially in that upper area, because of the slush." She frowned. "It was a rough winter. We had a lot of rain. Some weeks later I recall someone saying they thought our tortie, Audra, was gone. We all hoped she'd just found herself a home someplace. She was a sweet thing."

"Well, thank you, Peggy," Parker said. "Say, Savannah and Rags are leaving today; I'd better deliver her back to the condo so she can get her things together."

Peggy bowed slightly. "It's been an absolute pleasure meeting you beautiful and smart ladies. Thank you for all you've done for us and for the cats. Some of us are coming to Hammond, Savannah, to see the wonderful cat ranch you showed us in your video. And the ideas you gave us for fundraising and finding a major donor—priceless. We've already come up with some thoughts and strategies for projects and for approaching possible donors. Nancy Thornton and her husband own some property that just might work for the cats. It's actually in the national forest, but still close enough that we can continue keeping an eye on them."

"Super!" Savannah said.

"We're encouraged," Peggy said. She asked, "You're staying, Ms. Campbell?"

Parker nodded. "For a while longer. I still have work to do." She took Peggy's hand. "Thank you for your help. I'll see you soon." She started to step into her car when she realized that Savannah was still gazing across the colony.

"Peggy," Savannah said, "who owns this property? I think Parker told me the original landowner managed the colony here way back in the fifties or sixties. Did she deed the land over to you—to the street cat ladies?"

"I'm not sure of the legalities. I thought she did, but since our legal committee is concerned about losing this land to developers, I'm not so sure. There might have been a clause in there that the land reverts back to the heirs after a certain time."

"You have a legal committee?" Savannah asked.

"Yes," Peggy said. "I guess years ago there were complaints and even a lawsuit related to the cats and the property. That's when the legal committee was formed. We've followed that tradition throughout the years. I do know there's concern about developers—maybe actually not on this property, but close enough that it would disturb the cats."

Parker asked suspiciously, "Peggy, didn't the original colony gal—what's her name, Cora—didn't she lose her house and abandon her property because of it?"

"Yes," Peggy said. "Rumor has it that it was a giant mudslide. It took her house and some of the cats. Yes, the land was condemned, as I recall. If you can condemn land."

"I believe you can condemn it as unsafe to build on," Savannah said.

"So was it even legal for her to deed it over to you?" Parker asked. "Did she have that authority at the time?"

"Darn," Peggy said. "Good question. I must see what I can find out from the legal committee. They need to research those issues."

"Yes," Savannah said. "That could make all the difference for the future of your colony cats. It may be that you won't have to uproot them after all. I guess time and research will tell."

"What time do you expect to be home?" Parker asked later that morning when Savannah returned from her bedroom with her luggage.

"I have a lunch date with my friend, Rochelle, who lives not too far from here, then I'm headed home. I'll probably pull in around dinner time. How long will you stay?"

"For another few weeks," Parker said. "Houston will be here next week. I hope most of the unknown is behind us by then. I'll stay on to finish up the research and interview some of the colony ladies that we haven't met yet. I definitely want to follow up with the property issues. I may even do the writing while I'm here. I like the condo and the atmosphere." She pointed at Rags. "What does he have?"

"What?" Savannah asked, leaning over to see it. She picked up something off the floor. "Oh yes, Olivia and Rags found this out at the colony site, maybe yesterday or the day before. I put it in my pocket and planned to show it to the detective." She handed it to Parker. "Do you know what that is?"

Parker shook her head. "It's just a piece of plastic or something similar to plastic. It looks like it broke off of something." She examined it more closely and said, "I wonder what in the heck it is."

"I couldn't figure it out, but since the cats brought it to my attention…" Savannah started.

"I hear you," Parker said. "How about if I hold on to this? I hope to see the detective this afternoon. I'll show it to him."

"Great. Let me know," Savannah said.

"I will." Parker picked up Rags and rubbed her face against his. "Good bye, handsome. You take care. Hope to see you again soon." She lowered him to the floor and hugged Savannah. "This has been great—well, except for the nature of our project this week." She took a breath. "I think we made progress, though. You're great to work with, by the way."

"Well, thank you," Savannah said. "Likewise. I enjoyed myself—well, as you said, as much as one can enjoy themselves under circumstances like these." She kneeled next to Olivia, who was perched on the arm of a chair. "It was so fun getting to know you better, little missy." She kissed her cheek. "I will miss your sweet, sassy spirit, girl." She stood up and hugged Parker. "You, too."

Parker chuckled. "You'll miss my sassy spirit?"

"Sure will," Savannah said, hugging her again.

"Safe travels," Parker called as Savannah walked out to her car with Rags.

"So where are you taking me?" the detective asked after stepping into the car with Parker and Olivia later that day.

"On a most revealing hike," she said.

When she didn't elaborate, he looked into the backseat and said, "Hi, cat. That cat and her friend, Rags, are really something, the way they have helped us to focus on the smallest, yet sometimes the most significant things. We're often too busy trying to see the big picture, and they've reminded us that sometimes the big picture is in the smallest clue." He looked at Parker. "Does that make sense?"

"Kind of, I guess. Yes, the cats can be helpful in more ways than we realize. I just have to remember to listen to Olivia and tune into her reactions, no matter how subtle." She asked, "Is there anything new since we last talked?"

He shook his head. "Just more confirmation is all. I found another shoe—an expensive brand—and another one of those ads about that band." He turned to her. "Do you think that's significant?"

She shrugged.

After riding along in silence for a short while, Jud asked, "Do you know where you're going?"

"Yes. Savannah and I were here earlier, and I think you'll want to see what we found."

When he saw the cut fencing lying off to the side and began experiencing the bumps from the

238

deeply rutted road he said, "Parker, I don't think you're supposed to drive in here."

She grinned. "I can park and we can walk in." When he didn't respond, she said, "Anyway we're here."

"Where?" he asked, looking around.

"Come on, time for a hike." After a while, she asked, "Okay, do you know where we are now?"

The detective glanced around, then gazed into the distance. "Not really."

She pointed. "See that wooded area down there? That's the colony where the cats live."

He lifted his binoculars to his eyes. "Oh, yes, I can see that now." He lowered the glasses and asked, "You brought me up here because?"

"Did you know there was a mudslide up here right around seven years ago? My theory, and Savannah's, is that the hillside gave way on the night of January sixteenth and it caught eleven people or more unaware."

"What makes you think that?" he challenged.

"Research," she said. "And it wasn't easy. It went pretty much unnoticed."

Judson Caldwell slumped. He closed his eyes and muttered, "The night of January sixteenth? Oh, God."

"I'm sorry," Parker said, touching his arm compassionately. "I know this is hard for you."

239

He took a breath and said, "It's excruciating, but necessary. We need to know, especially those of us who lost a loved one that night." He took a couple of deep breaths and said, "A mudslide, huh? Makes perfect sense. But there's still one thing that doesn't make sense to me, and that is—as we discussed earlier—why? Why were they all here together—allegedly?" He looked around. "What would bring them to this spot?"

Parker shrugged, a wave of the horror those people must have experienced overtaking her. She took a breath and shoved her hand into her pocket. When she felt the item the cats had discovered she quickly pulled it out. "Detective, I think this could be an important clue, but I don't know what it means. The cats found it at the colony. Savannah took it from them day before yesterday, I believe. We both have a strong sense that it might be important, but we can't figure out what it came off of. See, it broke off of something. This side has rough edges. You're a tinkerer—a fixer of things. Do you know what that is?"

He took it from her and turned it over in his hands a couple of times, saying, "A small piece of curved plastic. Doesn't look important to me."

"So you don't know what it is or was?" she asked.

He took another look at it and said, "Yeah, actually I do know what it is. It's part of a finger pick—you know, for playing a guitar." He explained, "My nephew and some of his friends started a little garage band years ago. I had some musical background—in fact my mentor owned a music store—so I helped them get the equipment they needed. They were always losing and breaking picks. To this day I have a supply of them at home. One guy especially liked using finger picks, as opposed to the regular guitar picks."

Parker raised her eyebrows and spoke with more energy. "Well, that could explain a lot, don't you think so?"

"You lost me," the detective said impatiently.

"The reason those people were together up here that night. It was the music. I imagine that the Three Boy Band was playing. Why they played up here is a mystery that may never be resolved, but yeah, I imagine that's what brought that unlikely group of people together that night." Before the detective could speak, she said, "By the way, Savannah and I have another question."

He chuckled. "It seems that each discovery leads to more questions."

She nodded. "How did they get up here? Where are their cars? We saw only one mention of a car in all that paperwork you loaned us—I think it was in a newspaper article. It stated that Kaci Stuart's car was found a few miles away in the parking lot of a mini-mart days after she went missing."

"Right," he said. "I recall seeing that with the evidence. Now remember, some of those people were homeless; they may have taken public transportation to as close as they could get to the trailhead and they walked in from there."

"Makes sense," Parker said.

"I'm pretty sure there were other articles and maybe interview transcripts that mentioned cars eventually being found."

"Eventually?" Parker questioned.

"Well, sometime that week, I'd say."

"What about your daughter's car?" Parker asked quietly. "Was she driving that night?"

He shook his head. "She was grounded. Well, as far as the car was concerned. She'd had a couple of tickets, and my wife and I were trying to teach her a lesson. You know, one of those tough love things parents do that hurts them more than it hurts the child?" He added, "You probably don't know about that yet, since you don't have children."

"I have Olivia," she said, looking down at her as she sat at the end of her leash. "And I do know what you mean. I hate having to discipline her. She almost always gets her way." She asked, "So your daughter was on foot, or what?"

"I don't know. She left home on foot, but she may have met up with a friend down at the corner. You probably know how that goes," he said.

"That I do know. I was a teenager once," Parker quipped. More seriously, she asked,

242

"Detective, do you think there could be any cars under all that mud?"

He readjusted his baseball cap. "Gosh, I guess that depends on just how thick that stuff is." He surveyed the area and said, "From the looks of that divot in the hillside—I mean, that road's flat-out gone—I guess there could be a car or two down there. Cripes, it's just awful to imagine that happening to anyone." He closed his eyes and turned away.

Parker gave him a moment, then asked, "Do you remember there being any publicity about a mudslide up here around that time?"

"Vaguely. But it's not something I gave much thought to. I do remember hearing something about it, but it never occurred to me or evidently to anyone else, that people would have been up here that night. As far as the community was concerned, the slide was an inconsequential event. The focus was on the missing kids—that mudslide didn't even enter into the theories." He looked above them and below and shook his head. "My God. So that's how my little girl died?" He took a deep breath and walked away.

Parker sat down on a boulder with Olivia on her leash and let the detective grieve in private. When the cat pulled toward him she let her go and watched as Olivia rubbed against Judson Caldwell's leg. He picked her up and wept into her fur.

At that point, Parker could no longer hold back her emotions.

"Okay," the detective said several minutes later, standing up with Olivia in his arms, "I'd better get home and make some calls. It's time to involve the authorities, and I want to contact a few family members." He took her hand. "Thank you, Parker."

"For what," she asked, "for ruining your day?" She put a hand on his arm and said softly, "I'm so sorry."

"You didn't ruin my day," he said. "It's been hell for seven years. Finally I'll get closure."

"But…" Parker started.

"Yeah, she's gone. Now we can go on." He handed Olivia to her. "Thank you for loaning me your wonderful cat. It was nice having her to share my grief with. It's as if she understood."

"She does," Parker said, lowering Olivia to the ground and walking slowly with her and the detective back to the car.

The couple walked in silence for a few minutes, then the detective asked, "Why were the cats spared?"

"The colony cats?" Parker asked. "A sixth sense, maybe. Peggy told me a little while ago that she and the other ladies were aware of the mudslide mostly because the cats' dishes disappeared, but they didn't give it much thought. In fact, they didn't appear to be alarmed by the volume of mud that flowed down that night. It didn't seem to make as much of a noticeable impact on the terrain below as it did up here."

Later that evening as Parker worked on the outline for her article, her phone chimed. "It's the detective," she said out loud. "Hello, there. How are you this evening? Did you make your calls?"

"Yes," Jud said. "I called family, but I haven't alerted the captain to what we've discovered yet."

"Why?" Parker asked. "Are you concerned that you'll be in some sort of trouble for withholding evidence?"

"Naw," he assured her. "When the stuff started showing up we had no idea what it meant, where it came from, and how long it had been there. No, that's not my concern. Ms. Campbell," he said, "something has happened. Can you come over here and bring the cat, if you would?"

"Tonight?" she asked. "Is it urgent?"

"Yes," he said. "I've just uncovered evidence that my daughter might still be alive possibly in danger, but alive. Alive, Parker!"

"Oh my gosh, Jud. How…what…" she started. "Hey, listen, we'll be right there." She pocketed her phone, slipped into the jacket she hadn't taken time to hang up yet, and strapped

Olivia's harness around her. "Road trip, sweet girl. I think the detective has a job for you."

It didn't take Parker long to drive the distance to the detective's home. "Hmmm," she said, pulling into his yard. "I wonder if he's out in his shop or…oh, there he is waiting for us on the front porch. Come on, love-love. Let's go see what's going on. Hi!" she called, stepping out of the car with Olivia.

"Thanks for coming," he said. "I hope I didn't interrupt anything, but I just couldn't wait another minute, and you and the cat were the only ones I thought could help."

"What happened?" Parker asked, approaching.

He opened the front door and ushered her in. "Well, I did something I should have done a long time ago," he said, leading her down a hallway and into a small room.

Obviously a teenage girl's bedroom, Parker thought. "What did you do?" she asked gently.

"I snooped." Jud walked into the room and stopped. He turned to face Parker. "My wife died suddenly not too long after Hannah disappeared. She hadn't been well, and this just seemed to put her over the edge—to a place of no return. I haven't moved anything since my two best girls left me. I couldn't bear to disturb any of their things, until tonight. Tonight I charged my wife's phone, and then I drummed up the courage to look through it." He held a phone up in front of Parker. "This is a transcript of a message she got a few days after Hannah and the others went missing. Sally was already quite ill and not using her phone. I was busy and traumatized. I sure wasn't interested in hearing or reading messages from her girlfriends and the ladies at her church group and especially her annoying sister, but look what I found!" he exclaimed. "It's from Hannah. Parker, she's alive!" He frowned and said, "At least she was alive a few days after the mudslide or whatever happened on that hillside. She may have been in trouble, but alive."

Parker took the phone and read, "Mom, I'm okay. I'm with some new friends. They didn't want me to call anyone. They took my phone when they went into the mini mart, but they don't know how crafty I am thanks to Dad. Thanks, Dad. Brad left his phone charging in the car, so I'm on the floorboards using it. I just want to let you know I'm okay. I stupidly left my purse at their campsite. We tried to go back to get it, but the road was blocked off by mud. So far, I haven't had a reason to need my ID or anything; Brad and Travis pay for everything. It's a crazy situation, but I'm doing okay. Only they're being kind of weird about my privacy and I don't know what's up with that. Listen, I'm sure I'm okay, but if you don't hear from me in a few days you might want to come get me. Their information is hidden in my…"

She looked up at Jud.

"That's it," he said. "Obviously she didn't come back, and I need to find that information she hid." He looked down at Olivia. "I thought maybe she could help. You told me that she and that other cat—Savannah's cat—have a knack for finding things that might be important. And that just might be the most important thing I've ever needed to find." He choked up. "My daughter's life could be at stake."

"Oh my gosh," Parker said. "I just don't know…"

"Can you try?" Jud pleaded.

"Of course. Of course we will," she said. She looked down at Olivia. "Actually, she's already pulling against the leash."

"Take it off her!" he demanded excitedly.

Parker unfastened the leash and held on to Olivia. "Baby girl, see if you can find it. Find that information for the detective." She sat quietly with her eyes closed for a moment, then took her hands off Olivia and stepped back.

The couple watched as the pert calico sat down and looked up at Parker, then at the detective. She tilted her head, then stood up and walked toward the closet.

"I went through everything in there," Jud said. "And in her jewelry box, all of her drawers. Nothing."

Parker put her hand up to stop the detective. She said quietly, "Let her work. Give her a chance."

Shortly Olivia came out of the closet and lay down in front of a dresser. She peered underneath and reached in with one paw, then quickly stood up and jumped on top of the dresser. She sniffed around a small jewelry box, then hopped up onto the headboard and sniffed around, finally leaping onto a tall dresser. She pawed at the dresser scarf, uncovering a single hoop earring.

"Well, it doesn't look like my idea is going to work," Jud said. "I'm sorry to have bothered you, Parker."

"She's not finished," Parker said. "A cat isn't like a dog that goes straight to the clue or the lost child. A cat, I've noticed, works differently. At least Olivia does. She likes to drag things out—maybe add a little drama to the search."

They glanced wide-eyed at each other when Olivia leaped off the bed and ran back to the closet. She pawed at the door and Parker opened it. After a few moments, she pointed. "There! I think she has found something. It could be in that shoe box or under it."

The detective walked swiftly to where Olivia sat. He opened the shoe box and dumped out the contents. "Nothing here but shoes," he said. He turned the box over, then stuck a hand inside each of the shoes. "Maybe she's indicating *this* shoe box," he suggested, removing the lid from a second box and quickly examining the contents.

"No, look," Parker said. "Is that a loose board on the floor there?"

"Where?" Jud asked, anxiously.

Parker moved closer. "Ugh, everything's so dusty." She coughed a couple of times while moving a pair of sandals. She felt along the floor, finally asking, "Do you have a screwdriver or sturdy nail file—what about a pocketknife?'"

"Yeah," he said, producing a small knife.

Parker took it from him and used the blade to lift the board.

"Well, I'll be," Jud said. "She made herself a secret hiding place. I taught her that when she was six years old." He pointed at a flat-nose screwdriver hanging inside the closet door. "I wondered what that was for. As Hannah would say, 'Duh, Dad.'"

Parker chuckled. She pulled Olivia back out of the way and watched as Jud reached into the space and removed a small wooden box. "I'll bet she made this too," he said. He tenderly placed it on the smaller dresser and slowly opened the lid. He picked up a piece of paper on top and unfolded it. "Bingo," he said, pulling his phone out of his pocket.

"What are you going to do?" Parker asked.

"Place a call to the police station. I want an all-points bulletin out on these kidnappers."

"Wait," Parker suggested.

"What?" he asked, obviously annoyed.

"Think about it. Don't you want to be sure she's there, and that she needs help and isn't in danger before sending in a SWAT team?"

Jud sat down, rested his head in his hands. "All I want is my little girl home."

Parker sat down next to him and Olivia joined them, resting one paw on the detective's leg. He petted the cat.

"Yeah, I'm just about out of my mind," he said. "I've been on a damn rollercoaster of emotions for seven blasted years—especially these last few weeks. Do you know what that does to a father? It's been like a hell I've never experienced before." He ran his hand over Olivia and took a deep breath. "But I do believe you're right. I'd be saying the same thing to anyone else in this situation. 'Go slow. Know the particulars and the parameters. Think smart, not with emotion.'" He stood up. "Okay, here's what we'll do. I'll see what I can find out about these people and this address. I'll go over there tomorrow and see what kind of place it is and maybe get a glimpse of my daughter. I want to know everything about the situation before making my move."

"That sounds more reasonable," Parker said.

He nodded. "I know it does. You'll go with me, won't you? You and the cat?"

She grinned at him, and held out one arm. "Twist it," she said.

"What?" he asked.

"Twist my arm," she repeated.

He smirked at her and tried unsuccessfully to hold back a flow of tears. "I'm beginning to understand why I like you so much," he said. "You remind me an awful lot of my feisty daughter." He gave her a playful shove. "Now go get some sleep. I'll pick you up at six tomorrow morning."

Parker picked up Olivia and walked toward the front door. "We'll be ready."